Marble Wars

Granite Death Halls

(Episode II)

By Kevin J. Edwards

Acknowledgments

In a small rural town in Minnesota, I played Marble Wars many times quietly on the floor with marbles as a child when my mother was suffering from severe migraines after the loss of one of my brothers when he was only 13 years old to a nasty cancer. To share this childhood story with everyone is a lifelong dream fulfilment. It is an amazing accomplishment for me, as despite having a lot of education, I really struggle with spelling and writing well since those childhood days. I received a great deal of editing help from friends, family, and paid editor (through a grant from Five Wings Art Council) including: Tony Saler, Dave Schmitt, Carissa Andrews, Michelle Winter, and Ben Edwards. Christian Winter, with his mother's full consent, served as a target aged reader of the story, as he volunteered to listen and report his initial thoughts about Marbleman. In addition, Gabriel and Joe Edwards help to keep my writing dream alive by thinking of what it would be like to publish a book.

This book is dedicated to all of us with the brave hearts of all the hero's in Marble World!

Kevin J. Edwards, Ph.D., L.P.

Chapter 1
Methinks Spewing Spar

"I cannot believe any of this. I just can't believe it. I can't believe that my father, the King, all those innocence villagers, and the Stainless Steel Thunder guards have all been frozen. This just can't be happening. We shouldn't be hiding here in the barn. We should do something. What are we going to do?" asked Marbleman, as he nervously paced back and forth, shifting from human to marble form erratically.

"I don't know," answered his brother, Ironstone.

"I don't either but I don't think we should stay in this barn very long as everything bad that happened before started here. It is a good place to hide to after we saw all that horrible freezing, in the village" said Shuffle, as he rung his hands.

"I have an idea to save your father and rest of the frozen marbles," announced the old wizard, Moss Agate.

"Hey everybody, look over there, in the distance," interrupted Shuffle Boy.

They all stepped over to peer out the old crack in the barn wall.

"There is that filthy rat Menacing Strong. Let's get him," said Marbleman, as his friends grabbed his arms to hold him back. "Hey, let go of me. We should have never rolled back here to the barn to hide. We should've attacked him right there in the village, when we had the chance."

"We did not stand a chance then, nor do we now. Don't you think I want to avenge our father as much as you do, my brother? Just look at his army rolling with him. There are thousands with him. We cannot possibly take them all. If they freeze us too, we will be no good to rescue father. The old wizard says he has a plan. Listen to him, Marbleman. We will avenge our father," encouraged Ironstone.

Again, Shuffle Boy interrupted, "Hey, look way over there, in the far distance to the valley leading east. It looks like a wagon full of the frozen. Maybe your father and the King are in there?"

Marbleman tightened his eyes and blinked several times to focus on the wagon so far away. "I think you're right, I can see something in the back of the wagon. Where are they taking them?"

Putting one hand on Marbleman's shoulder, Moss Agate said, "They are taking the frozen to Granite Death Halls to hide them where nobody will ever find them."

"What the blam damsel, anyway," shouted Marbleman. Once again, he nervously paced the barn floor back and forth, shifting from human to marble form. "We must hurry to stop them." With tears forming in his eyes, he shook his head back-and-forth, and mumbled, "How can I let them take my poor old father to the infamous dungeons of Granite Death Halls? That is no place for my sweet old dad."

"All is not lost. I must confess something to you. I am very familiar with many of the secret passageways in Granite Death Halls, as I once walked those passages freely," said Moss Agate. "I do have a plan. We can sneak in there to unfreeze your father and everyone else. I know of a way to get in."

Menacing Strong's armies were out of sight when Moss said, "Come with me Marbleman, I must show you something that will help rescue your father. Just you. Let's go outside."

Marbleman followed the old agate by lowering his head to squeeze under the broken split barn door as the top half no longer opened. "Rats I almost made it" he thought as one broken board caught his brown leather battling suit making him stumble out of the barn right on his face. Pulling himself off the ground he called out ""Mr. Agate sir, where the heck did you go already?"

"No wonder I can't see him there is so much overgrowth. The years have not been good to this old farmyard. There weeds, bushes, and trees are out of control. Its really a sorry sight for a farm," thought Marbleman.

His thoughts were broken when a overgrown branch slapped him directly in the face as he attempted to move past it to fine the old agate. He cried out "Ouch, that does it, were are you old goat?"

"Right over here my young apprentice." Moss returned as he lazily sat the end of a broken fence post facing a small clearing that must have been an open pasture at one time. "This is enough open space to teach you what I need to today." He continued.

Marbleman stepped over the broken fence and faced Moss. From underneath his cape, Moss Agate brought out an elegant looking freezing blade. "Here, take this tool of justice. It is from your father. It is not an ordinary freezing sword. It has powers only one true king can bring forth. Go ahead, take it. It's yours," said Moss Agate, as he held it up for Marbleman. "Do you know what this is?"

"Yes, methinks that's your Spewing spar. Remember, I saw you use it before," said Marbleman.

"Wrong. This is your Spewing Spar," said Moss.

"What?" said Marbleman, surprised.

"That's right. This exceptional weapon is yours, passed down to you by your real biological father, the King," said Moss.

"First of all, you keep telling me my real father is the King. You know that is really hard to believe. Back in my village I was raise by my father Gemstone Landroller, a common village marble, not a king. I know you told me that the King placed me there in Gemstone's care for my own good. But it's also hard to believe," explained Marbleman. "Second of all, I can't begin to use that thing. Everyone knows only those with special abilities can wield a Spewing Spar."

"It's all true. You're right. Only those with inborn exceptions and battling skills can wield it. And that is you Marbleman. You are born of royalty. You have many unique skills that will blossom out of you. Let me show you. There is much I need to teach you. I'll prove it to you right now. Catch," replied Moss, as he threw the special weapon in the air to Marbleman.

"Whoa, you got to be kidding," said Marbleman, as he caught the blade wrapped in its sheath with his left hand and quickly pulled it out with his main battling right hand.

Wow, it does seem to fit me like a glove, he thought, as his fingers explored the handle of the blade.

"You have the royal right to wield this Spewing Spar sword. You have yet to discover the powers within you. If you let me, I will help guide you, as the Manifest Power of Peace is strong with you. Now concentrate. Command the weapon with your mind," instructed Moss.

"Really, speak to a blade with my mind?" Marbleman said, as he lowered his chin shaking his head back and forth in skepticism.

What the heck? Okay, Spewing Spar, show me your stuff, he thought. With that, the Spewing Spar lit up and began spitting small flashes of freezing blots. *Well that's cool but not too much power...* Before he could finish his thought the sword's freezing light rays thundered, divided into two, and then subdivided into six huge, long freezing lightening-like bolts dancing and quivering in the air all around Marbleman.

"Whoa, nooooo," he shouted, as he quickly returned his new Spewing Spar, with all of its freezing light streams, back into its sheath. "Holy marble cows. What just happened?"

"I could have frozen myself. Did you see all those freezing bolts? I couldn't control them," he said to Moss.

Running toward him, with their freezing blades drawn, both Ironstone and Shuffle Boy charged to Marbleman's apparent rescue.

"What happened? Where is the fight? We heard freezing blade thunder and saw colored lights in the sky," said Ironstone.

Moss Agate laughed. "It's all right. You're two protectors of the King's son. But your friend is only beginning to learn about his Spewing Spar," replied Moss.

Ironstone's eyes widened as he did a double take. First to his bother and then to the old agate. "What? You mean my brother can wield a Spewing Spar?" he asked Moss Agate.

"Of course. As I told you, your bother is of royal blood. But even more than that, the Manifest Power of Peace runs strong through out the very essence of his entire soul."

"Wow, way cool bro. Way to go," said Ironstone, as he pretended to slug his brother in the stomach.

"Hey, wait a minute… Does this mean he is a wizard, like you? You said something before about only wizard can control Spewing Spars," said Shuffle Boy, as he took a couple of steps backward from everybody.

"Ah, my young little friend, you are wise beyond your years. There are different kinds of wizards. Your friend here is of a kind of wizard called the Masterminds," replied Moss Agate.

"Yeah, so what does that exactly mean?" said Shuffle.

"Be not afraid my little friend. I can't tell you everything about Masterminds right now, as their history runs deeps, but what you need to know is they don't rely on anything from the dark Power of War. Instead, they get all their power from their highly developed minds and outstanding genius to summons and control the positive forces all around us, from the Manifest Destiny of the Power of Peace. Yes, my little friend, this includes the ability to command fighting weapons, like this Spewing Spar," explained Moss.

Ironstone asked, "How many more are there like my brother?"

"I am afraid not many more exist, as they're kind is disappearing. Your brother is special, as we have been waiting for new blood to bring hope to the return of the Mastermind race. Marbleutopia has been vulnerable to be taken over by those from the Manifest Power of War. If this happens, darkness will fall upon all of Marble World. It will be horrors like we have never seen. Menacing Strong and his Furious Forces are looking for your brother, since Menacing has felt a shift in the Manifestation of Powers. This shift threatens his plans of taking over Marbleutopia," said Moss, as his eyebrows lowered and his smile disappeared.

"How does he know my brother is the new Mastermind blood?" questioned Ironstone.

Moss quickly replied, "Prophecy has long foretold of the new blood coming from royal bloodline. Menacing Strong believes this knowledge of the future, as he too once was deeply connected with the Power of Peace. He was the Master Chief of the Masterminds, many years ago, before he turned to the evil side and tied to overthrow King Trueround."

"What?" shouted Marbleman. "He can't be of the same kind of blood as me. Menacing is the meanest being in this world and the World Above. He has no mercy, just like when froze my brother and me. If wasn't for Shuffle we probably be stacked away in Granite Death Halls with everyone else."

"Yes, and it's a good thing he only thought you were a lowly marblerat from the village. If he knew who you truly were, he would have cracked you and your brother to death," spoke Moss, solemnly.

Looking directly into Marbleman's eyes, Moss said, "Now you can understand why your biological father sent you to live with Gemstone. Right? Menacing vowed to harm you and your mother, the king's wife. All of Marbleutopia went into deep despair when your mother disappeared. She's never been found. Everyone suspected Menacing of taking her. That's when the King sent you away in the middle of the night to be raised in secret in Glory Village. You were just a small child."

"Hey, my mother, the queen, she could be frozen in Granite Death Halls. Why didn't the king attack and search that dirty old place?" asked Marbleman.

"The King desperately wanted to do just that and tear apart every brick of that citadel looking for his queen. But you have seen the vast number of allies Menacing Strong has under his control. Nobody in the Kings land knew fore sure what happened to Menacing but he was presumed to be frozen somewhere after the last confrontation or was in hiding from the kings wrath. Your father did not want to start a war of all wars to jeopardize all the life in Marbleutopia for his own needs. All those evil allies of Menacing in the outer rim of remained loyal to him and they too, someday want their own piece of Marbleutopia. And that's exactly what would happen, war, if the king waged war against Menacing's fortress. Besides, he was not absolutely sure it was Menacing that made your mother disappear. But he's never stopped looking for her."

Marbleman heard in his head those terrifying words of Menacing's ringing loudly; *The Manifest Power of War is ours. I have the power. Onward to Marbleutopia, it and its crown is ours for the taking.*

Marbleman's eyebrows scrunched as he moved close to Moss and said, "Teach me everything you know."

"My pleasure, young prince. First of all, be not afraid of your Spewing Spar. It has already bonded with you. If it had not bonded with you, it would not have fired up."

"Do you mean this Spewing Spar can think? That it has a mind of its own?" questioned Marbleman.

"I know it's hard to believe that a weapon has a mind of its own, but through the mystical Power of Peace, it does act on its own at times," replied Moss. "This Spewing Spar is your talisman. It will not only fight for you and protect you in battle against evil with its mystical powers, it will also bring you good fortune in all your travels."

Ironstone leaned forward and said, "We need all the help and luck we can get if we are going to Granite Death Halls."

"Speaking of help," Moss said, as he turned to Shuffle Boy. "I hear you're fast."

"Yes sir, I am the fastest," replied Shuffle.

"Shuffle Boy, I have an utmost import task for you, and you must not fail," he said to the young friend. "You must warn Marbleutopia that war is upon them. Go as fast as you can. Get word to the four generals of Marbleutopia, warning them of Menacing's attack. Marbleutopia has not been at war for many centuries. They will be caught off guard, if you can't get there in time. You must roll to Marbleutopia faster than Menacing Strong can get his army there."

Putting a hand on Shuffle's shoulder, Marbleman said, "Remember how you burned up Championship Cascading Runs?"

"I'll never forget," replied Shuffle.

"Now is your chance to use your speed again, as you must get to the generals before Menacing. Don't be seen or get captured. You can do this Shuffle," encouraged Marbleman.

"But you need me to help you in getting everyone out of Granite Death Halls," complained Shuffle.

"You heard the old agate. It is more important that Marbleutopia be warned. The armies of Menacing have a big start on you headed to the city. We will figure out Granite Death Halls," said Marbleman. "There's no one else in all the World Below that can make it happen."

Shuffle Boy, listening with all seriousness, said, "There are too many of them to move fast through the chutes and forest. But I can beat them to the city. I know I can." Without another word, he nodded his head, turned to shift into his fast marble form, and was gone.

Ironstone shouted after Shuffle Boy, "May the Power of Peace be with you!"

To which he heard a faint reply in the distance, "And peace be with you!"

Marbleman turned to his brother with authority, "Now, my brother, this is our time. We must save our father and King. When we have them safely unfrozen, we will give Menacing Strong a battle he will never forget."

Moss Agate said, "I know of a side entrance with only a few guards. One guard in particular, we can bribe. His name is Gobbledygook. He is a low life, son of a marble horse thief. He is very odd. Whatever you do, do not trust him. I am afraid this is all I can offer, as once inside, it is a maze of dark passages with locked cells scattered throughout. Your fathers and the others could be hidden frozen anywhere deep in the halls. Be warned, there are dungeon guards, traps we do not want to fall into, and evil creatures we do not want to face."

"Traps?" echoed Ironstone.

"Evil creatures. Are you trying to scary us away?" questioned Marbleman.

"I don't want to scare you, but you need to be prepared for the worse," said Moss.

Wow, my life is changing. Is all this true?" thought Marbleman. *Am I really the King's son, the heir to the throne, and the Glory Crown? I think I am. I can feel it now.*

"What about my lessons?" asked Marbleman.

"I will teach you on the way. Time is essential now," answered Moss.

I can feel it sweeping through my bones, knowing I must not only save my fathers against the evil forces of Menacing Strong, I must save Marbleutopia and the whole World Beneath from falling to the dark Manifest Power of War, Marbleman thought. *I cannot stand around anymore. I must save them.*

"Let's roll to Granite Death Halls and save my fathers," commanded Marbleman with determination.

Chapter 2
River Lessons

"Are we there yet?" asked Marbleman, turning to Moss Agate in all seriousness.

Ironstone spoke softly to his brother as they continued to roll hard and fast, "We have never been this far in the outer rim and it's getting dark. How far off is Granite Death Halls anyway?"

Moss overheard the brothers. "You're right, we are far your home. These are dangerous lands in the outer rim. Many are loyal to Menacing Strong in these parts. Our enemies can be anywhere. You need to be careful of all we encounter."

"What do you mean? There are more enemies than Menacing Strong and his armies?" questioned Ironstone.

"You already saw the Red Rogues and Blue Tyrannicals aid in the attack against your village with Menacing Strong and his personal Furious Forces army. There could be more of any of them spread though out these lands. But worse yet, are Corsoes. They think their skin color is superior over all others, with the deep mixed colors of bright red and blue. They pride themselves in being the meanest clan of marble people."

"Great, just what we need. More nasty clans of enemies. Aren't there any good souls in these parts? I just can't believe everyone around her is bad," said Marbleman.

"Yes, we are not alone. In fact, I have word out for some good clans to come to are aid. I have not heard from them yet, but I believe they will come," said Moss. "We can rest at the river, which is just ahead, and I will teach you more about your weapon, Marbleman."

"More water," said Ironstone. "No wonder father told us to be careful of water. It is everywhere in these parts."

"Aw yes, this is no ordinary river either. It will be our path to the seldom used gateway to Granite Death Halls. As you know, we don't care for water too much, so everyone avoids this path to the halls. This river runs deep into and under the dungeons.

You need to be wary of this river inside the halls, as it lets no one go who falls within its currents. It is a muddy fate for all that get trapped. Worse yet, it is known to be patrolled by a hideous flying monster, to make sure no one ever gets out of the water's muddy abyss beneath the fortress. There are hundreds, if not thousands, who are stuck there for life," warned Moss.

"Geez, this adventure is just getting better and better," said Ironstone, as he rolled his eyes and shook his head back and forth. He rolled up to the river edge, shifting into his human form, along with the others.

The brothers gave each other sideways glances, looking at the river, when Moss said, "Go ahead, you can clean your shells here, as the water is shallow, and the bottom is sandy. We can enjoy this part of the river." With that, he stepped into the river.

"Actually, the water is not all that bad," said Marbleman, lifting his hands full of water to pour on his head.

All three of the boys giggled like children at finding enjoyment in the water. However, they were abruptly stopped as Moss Agate spoke very seriously as he said, "I have more to tell you. It's a rather long story, and I hope you will not think less of me, as I know the Granite Death Halls very well, as I use to live there."

Ironstone grabbed his brother's shoulder, pulling him backward away from Moss.

Marbleman spoke bluntly, "Hey, you hinted about that before, about knowing things in Granite Death Halls and knowing Menacing Strong. You're not in cahoots with Strong as old pals are you? We thought you were here to help us. After all, we have trusted you to take us this far."

"I am here to help you. Please just hear me out, because I don't want this secret to become between us someday," he said, moving in circles, as he waded around the brothers.

"Well, go on, then. Speak your piece," replied Marbleman.

Moss began, "When I was a young apprentice scientist, many millenniums ago, I was selected by the wisest marbles in my village to attend a private academy for the study of the Manifest Destiny of Peace. The academy was located in a faraway palace, away from everything, to reduce distraction from studying. In those days, it was just call

Granite Halls. Unfortunately, it would be many years later, that the academy's name would be changed to reflect the evilness within those walls."

Moss abruptly sat on a nearby rock protruding out of the water. His gaze lowered to stared at the gentle flow of the river around his legs.

"Aw, old man, that must have been hard times for you when everything changed," consoled Marbleman.

"Yes, it brings such great sadness to my heart to watch a place I loved turn to a malevolent building," he said, as his gaze met Marbleman's. Moss continued, "It was not a bad place in the beginning; no far from it. In the beginning, when I went there as a young apprentice, it was for the study of controlling one's own thoughts to a deeper level, far beyond the surface of everyday thinking. It was a celebrating of intelligence and only for the power of good things. The mind is powerful. But when you combine it with the natural forces of our universe, it becomes even more powerful. We were learning how to communicate with seen and unseen things, including special weapons that were crafted to hear and follow commands to protect the innocent. These early teachings were about using our mind's powers to help promote peace and prosperity. At the time, they called all students at academy Apprentice Masterminds. It was an in-depth study, or if you will, a devotion to the study of The Manifest Destiny and the Power of Peace."

"Gee whiz, that sounds like it was such a good place. How in the world did it become such an evil place now?" questioned Marbleman.

"Yes, yes, yes, such a good place. Why, many noble marble people were educated there and went on to accomplish great things for Marble World," replied Moss.

"Like who?" asked Ironstone, who positioned himself on anther rock, facing Moss Agate.

"Well there was one who stood out above the others. He was very clever in discerning between right and wrong. He was high in the character of the mind and was a descendant from a long line of nobility. His name is Virtuoso Trueround."

"Do you mean, King Trueround?" asked Marbleman.

"That's right. When he first became king of Marbleutopia, he had many Mastermind advisers traveling to him. They helped him keep on a path of goodness and to build the great city to what it is now," explained Moss.

Wow, there is so much in my family history to learn. I never knew any of this stuff. This is super interesting, Marbleman thought to himself.

Moss continued, "However, over time, many began to be suspicious of the King's advisors because they came from so away in the outer rim of our world. For those didn't understand the purpose of the academy, they became fearful of what was going on inside the hall and questioned the advice given to the king. The fearful were so skeptical; they began to associate Mastermind studies to the evil side of wizardry and magic. Perhaps it was like a self-fulfilling prophecy as, alas, over time this became true. The change really became true because of one Chief Mastermind, who was the most trusted advisor and best friend to your father. He led some to change to the study of the Manifest Power of War."

Marbleman stood still in the river, as his eyebrows curled against each other. He abruptly slapped the water hard once with his right hand and then again with his left. He looked to the night sky and yelled, "Menacing Strong, you traitor."

Moss calmly continued with his story, "When Trueround became the King, my mentor's marble heart, yes it was Menacing Strong, began to change for the worse. He was jealous of the King. In truth, he was angry he was not chosen to be King. Hiding his feelings, he worked side-by-side with Trueround, as his trusted right-hand marble for ages. Almost overnight, Menacing Strong turned from studies of good to studying the dark side of the powers around us. He wanted to find a way to become king, even if it meant using force against his lifelong friend. He was consumed with thoughts of not only being the king, but also of being all-powerful. He felt marble people did not know what was good for them. It was in the Manifest Power of War, where he found hope to realize his dream. He turned to the malevolent side. My mentor began to change all of his students thinking to his evil side Manifest Power of War, except one. That one was me. I left my studies at Granite Halls because it was becoming ugly and full of hatred."

This is new, thought Marbleman, as he saw and felt goose pimples surging all over his body. *It is the Manifest of Peace. I can feel it.*

Marbleman could see the tears streaming down Moss's tired, old-looking face when Moss said, "Excuses me a minute, I need to gather myself. He got up from his rock perch, walked to the riverbank, shifted into his round form, and slowly rolled into the woods, leaving the two brothers in the river.

"Holy cows, brother. What do you think about all of that?" question Ironstone. "I did not know there was such a deep hatred inside of Menacing Strong," replied Marbleman. "Brother, look at all the goose pimples on my arms. I feel the Power moving through me."

"Powerful feelings, are they not?" replied a voice was that was sweet and alluring.

"Hey" said Marbleman as one of his vision at the Assumption pool was standing right next to him and she began caressing his arm lowering his goose bumps. *This is no vision she is real,* he thought. "Who are you," he demanded.

"You know who I am. am the girl of your dreams, Desiree Sapphire. But you can just call me Fire," she said, as she seductively stroked his arm.

Before Marbleman could reply, yet another enchanting female voice came directly behind his brother saying, "Ironstone, I have been watching you for a long time and have been waiting for you."

Ironstone turned his head to look toward the voice, as he remained sitting on his rock. His mouth dropped wide opened, his eyebrows lifted to full height, as his pupils widened to the max. Standing before him was the most gorgeous female marble he had ever seen. Not knowing what to say, he repeated his bothers question, as he barely choked out, "Who are you?"

"You must know me, aren't I the girl of your dreams? Why, I am the sister of Fire. My name is Allure Sapphire," she said, rubbing his shoulder muscles, as he sat frozen on the rock, just as if a freezing blade had stuck him.

Marbleman shouted to Allure, "Hey, how do you know my brother's name?"

Fire placed her left hand on Marbleman's face to steer his eyes directly into hers, as she softly said, "Why everyone knows of the famous brother's coming of age story, Marbleman, heir to the throne. Of course you'd be with your faithful brother, Ironstone, to the end of the worlds. You are protectors of all of Marble World and the World Above, according to prophecy."

I must not black out. What can I do? thought Marbleman, as his sensual feelings were racing a full speed through his brain. *I can't stop quivering. It must be the cold water. Yes, yes it must be this frigid water. Nope, who am I kidding? It is her. I am shaking like a leaf in the wind due to her. She is fantastic looking. She is fire alright; she is smoking hot.*

Fire moved in even closer placing her hand over Marbleman heart as she rose up to his ear on her delicate tippy-toes whispering, "Come with me my love to a place where we will never grow old together. Come with me to Tir-na-nog a magical place were your dreams come true. Together with your royal bloodline, might, wisdom, and me at your side we will rule all of Marble World and then all the World Above. I can make all your dreams come true. You will be my king and I will be your queen forever" she cooed.

"Hey, both of you hussies get away from them. You shall not scramble their hearts," shouted Moss Agate from the riverbank.

Thank goodness, thought Marbleman, as he jolted back to some of his regular senses.

With her free right hand, Fire stole Marbleman's Spewing Spar right off his hip. It left his leather holster without Marbleman knowing it was taken. She moved fast toward the far side of the riverbank with her sister, away from the brothers and especially away from the old Mastermind.

"You're too late, old wizard," Fire triumphantly yelled back, as she waved Marbleman's Spewing Spar above her head. "And boys, don't be mad at us; we will be back for you," she added as both sisters blew air kisses to the brothers, before they disappeared into the heavy brush.

"You knucklehead. You let her steal your spewing spar. Come on, shake off their hypnotic spell. Quickly, get after those deceitful evil enchantresses. We must get your weapon back," commanded Moss as he swiftly crossed the river, climbed the riverbank, shifted into his fast marble rolling form, and he too disappeared into the heavy brush not waiting for the brothers.

"Come on, brother," Marbleman called out to Ironstone.

Plowing through the river, Marbleman reached the bank where Moss climbed out, only to hear, "Help, brother." Marbleman turned quickly to see his brother struggling in the water just as his head went under.

Rapidly, Marbleman strode through the water to his brother. "Oh my," he said aloud. *It's a muddy drop off. I must not sink in or I won't be able to help Ironstone or myself,* he thought. Sliding his foot on the riverbed, he felt for the edge of the drop off. "Grab my hand," he shouted, hoping his brother could hear him under the water as he thrust his hand downward. "Got ya," he hollered.

Ironstone's downward momentum pulled him toward the sinkhole. Struggling to rescue his brother, Marbleman swore, "Blam Damsel it anyway. Come on, *pull,*" he cried out, as he planted his rear foot in the sand to pull out the other from sliding into the hole.

Fighting and pulling to get his brother out of the water, he fell backward and sat, completely submerged, on the river bottom, with an iron fist grasp on his brother's hand. Marbleman chopped his feet back and forth to get a strong foothold in the sandy part of the river to pull his brother out.

I always wondered how time stood still in emergency situations, as others have said. But I feel it now, everything feels like slow motion. I am going to die right here under the water. I am going to drown. I am running out of breath. Wait, marble people don't drown. Is it true what father said; that marble people can breathe under water? I am afraid. I really don't want to find out this way. I can't hold my breath any longer. But I must not let go of my brother, he thought. *Here it goes.*

"Gasp," was the involuntary sound that escaped his mouth, as the water rushed in, filling his human insides. He watched the last air bubbles escape from his mouth, and then surprisingly, he breathed.

Yahoo! How cool is this? I can breathe under water. And my vision is pretty clear too, he thought, spotting Ironstone.

"I see you my brother," Marbleman said aloud under the water.

"How about that? I hear and see you too. How cool is this? I just can't move very well under here. I am stuck in this slippery muddy slope," replied Ironstone.

"Keeping work together. We'll get you out of this muddy hole," said Marbleman, as the two brothers scrambled their way out of the sinkhole, until they sat soaking wet on riverbank.

"Thanks bro," said Ironstone. "Hey, what's with your face? What are you smiling about? You look like you just received the best present in your life."

I am so grateful I did not lose you. You're my brother. I would die for you. I need my brother forever, thought Marbleman. But instead, he slapped Ironstone on the back and joked, "Just stop messing around. No more silly swimming lessons in the middle of rivers full of sinkholes. We can't waste anymore time. We need to find that old agate and get my weapon back from those Sapphire temptress sisters. Come on. Let's get out of here."

Chapter 3
Allies and Enemy Conundrums

"Let's go," said Marbleman, as he and his brother stood up from the riverbank and looked into the deep thicket of the forest.

"But go where?" said Ironstone. "Where did the old agate go? Which way? You know we don't exactly have any idea where we are going. We have never been on this side of the river. Not to mention, nighttime sure seems to come fast when we have been rolling all day. Plus, we only have the firestreaks in the night sky to see by. It's way too dark to see well. I don't know what to do brother. Do you?"

"I don't know either. I do know we need to be extra careful, though, as we are now on the eastside of the river. We have entered the outer rim and the vast area that is under Menacing's thumb. Remember the old agate said there are many allies that are loyal to Menacing Strong here. Probably spies, too. I wish I had my spewing spar now. It's really beginning to grow on me," answered Marbleman.

"Where is your regular freezing blade? I still have mine," said Ironstone.

"Oh, you probably didn't see, but the old agate made me hide my old freezing blade in the barn just before we left. He said I had to learn to trust only one weapon, so I'd have to use my Spewing Spar from now on. He kind of acted like the Spewing Spar has a mind of its own and that it would get, well, jealous if I used other weapons. Weird right?" Marbleman said.

"That *is* weird," replied Ironstone, as he with drew his freezing blade to step into the forest. Loud laughter and noisy voices broke the silence, like a party was going on, not far from them. Ironstone shifted his gaze to Marbleman. "That doesn't sound like the old agate or those sisters."

"Well, I guess we know where we are going now. Let's check it out. But be very quiet until we figure out what is going on," said Marbleman.

It only took a few steps, stumbling and fighting to get through the thicket, when Ironstone whispered, "I don't think we will sneak up on anyone with all this rustling of branches we make with every step."

"Shush. Keep going, but be quiet, for the love of Pete sake," commanded the elder brother.

Ironstone whispered extra quietly, "I see a light from a fire right over there. Come on we can get close for a good look."

"Look at that would you? A campsite. There sure are a lot of marble people hanging around. Do you think they're the enemy? Or in league with Menacing's side? Or could they be those allies for us that the old agate said where supposed to be coming to help?" whispered Ironstone.

"Shush. How would I know who is who?" Marbleman whispered back.

Ironstone continued whispering only loud enough for his brother to here, "Wow, that's really a big clearing right here in the middle of the woods. What are they all doing way out here? Do you think there are more of them in those tents spread around? Look right by the fire, an old man cooking in that big old pot. Actually, that smells real tasty for my human side appetite. The campfire smoke is getting kind of heavy but of what I can see of him he looks nice enough."

Just then, the older looking marble person sitting on a log by the fire, with a hood covering most of his face, raised his head and looked right through the smoke directly at the brothers in their hiding spot in the weeds.

The elder said, "Come over here my sons, be not afraid. Your destiny awaits you here by the campfire. We have been expecting you."

Ironstone shot a quizzical look at Marbleman and said, "Well, it's your call."

"They all seem friendly enough. Holster your weapon, brother, and we will find out what he means by expecting us. Because, I was certainly not expecting him. Besides, we don't exactly have a place to run to," answered Marbleman.

Slowly the brothers sauntered out of the brush to approach the campfire. The others in the camp did not seem to pay any attention to the brothers, as they continued on their own tasks.

"Come closer, closer, closer," said the old hooded marble to the brothers. Once beside the fire, the elder marble smiled widely, as he removed his hooded cloak to reveal his whole face.

"Oh, noooo, it's Jasper," shouted Marbleman, backing way and grabbing his brother's arm to pull him backwards with him.

"The wizard, Moss Agate, told us to stay away from you," added Ironstone.

"Blam damsel it anyway, this was a trap," said Marbleman, as he looked to the right and left, seeing all the others in the camp were now fully focused on, and encircling the brothers with their freezing blades drawn. "Oh geez, look brother. There are Red Rouges and Blue Tyrannicals, just like the ones we saw attack our village. I don't know who those blue and red mixed ones are, but they don't look friendly at all."

Ironstone drew out and lit up his freezing blade as, the two put their backs together while moving in circle fashion, in an attempt to watch everyone moving towards them.

"Stay close brother, I will fight them off as long as I can," shouted Ironstone.

"There are too many of them. We are not going to make it through this one," said Marbleman, under his breath.

"This is your lucky day," yelled Jasper, as he moved in front of everyone in the inner circle.

"Ho, ha, ha, ho," went the laughing evil crowd, of which all seemed to be having a great time at taunting the circled prey. The evil numbers grossly overmatched the two brothers.

"It's your lucky day because your friends over there want me to show mercy on you by freezing you swiftly to minimize the pain. They promised they will personally take care of your frozen shells, by taking you to Granite Death Halls and hiding you in a real good place," cajoled Jasper.

Marbleman shook his head back and forth in disbelief, as the Sapphire sisters were waving to him from behind their entrapment circle.

"Yoo-hoo boys. Jasper is right. We will take real good care of you. You'll be safely hidden, so no bad animals or anything will interrupt your peaceful, frozen sleep.

But one thing before you go sweethearts, tell me how do you get this thing to work?" Desiree cooed waving his Spewing Spar above her head.

"Come on over here. I'll show you and I promise to personally take care of you," shouted back Marbleman.

This banter brought another hardy round of laughter from the crowd.

"Enough already. I, nor Menacing Strong, can have a possible heir to the throne running around spoiling our plans," Jasper said, as he lit his Spewing Spar, and raised it as high as his arm could reach upward. Two large bolts of freezing lighting zoomed straight up in the sky and then bent downward, as he aimed it directly at the brothers.

"Lookout," called out Marbleman, shoving his brother away from the freezing bolt strike and barely avoiding being struck himself.

"Arggh," growled Jasper, clearly disgusted that he missed both brothers. He sent another round of more intense freezing bolts, with one bolt reaching Ironstone first.

"Not his time," cried out Ironstone, as he blocked the steady freezing stream with his own freezing blade. "Oh no." The power of the steam turned a dark blue, and drove him to the ground until he was flat on his back.

"Hang on brother," screamed Marbleman.

What can I do? he thought.

But it was too late, as the second freezing stream launched upward, then downward again, straight for him.

"Noooo," came out of his mouth, as instinctively, he held out his hand in front of his face in an attempt to deflect the freezing blast.

"Not on my watch," said Moss Agate from somewhere behind the circle of foes. His Spewing Spar bolt met and blocked Jasper's freezing stream in mid-air, blocking it mere inches in front of Marbleman's face.

"Whoa," said Marbleman, as he was knocked to the ground from the thunder made by the two Spewing Spars' strength colliding with each other. "Pretty loud, huh?" he said to a Red Rouge, who was knocked to the ground right next to him. His eyes focused on the foe's freezing blade, which landed beside him. "I'll take that," he said, as he grabbed the enemy's freezing blade and with one quick, decisive blow the Red Rouge froze instantly before him. "Sorry."

Simultaneously, the old agate's freezing stream knocked away and extinguished a new freezing stream aimed at Ironstone. "Get up both of you and get that Spewing Spar from those temptresses," commanded Moss, as he squared off for a wizard duel with Jasper.

"Come on, brother," encouraged Marbleman, as they got to their feet and moved toward the sisters.

After only a few steps forward, Ironstone's enthusiasm for a fight dropped, as he said, "Ohhhh boy." Dozens of enemies closed ranks, blocking their path to the sisters.

"Come on brother, let's show them what we can do," called out Marbleman, as the brothers charged right at the dozens of Red Rouges and Tyrannicals standing in their way.

"Okay, but there sure are a lot of them," said Ironstone, followed by bellowing, "Aarghhhhh," as his battle cry.

Just then, Moss Agate, diverted his attention from Jasper, as he lifted his brown satchel off his shoulder and raised it to the sky. Then, throwing it hard to the ground, he roared, "I open your passage."

The booming blast from the satchel sent out thousands of freezing shards in every which way.

"Oh no," and "You've got to be kidding me," squawked from dozens of enemies, as the freezing shards hit their target.

"Blam damsel," howled Desiree. "I have never seen anything like that before." Suddenly, a clear path was now made between the sisters and brothers.

As the smoke from the blast lifted, Jasper stood in the far corner of the campsite and called out, "Got to hand it to you, old agate. You still have a few good tricks up your sleeve. Alas, I would love to stay an see what other tricks you have up your sleeve but I don't have the time as duty calls me elsewhere, so until next time." With that, he shifted into his faster marble form, and zipped into the dense dark forest, with a handful of other enemies, who avoided being frozen.

"I'll take that," Marbleman said, pointing to his freezing weapon in Desiree's hand.

"Oh dear me… I just don't know what to do. I do so need you Marbleman, and your little sword, too. We belong to together. It is our destiny," faked Desiree, as if she was now from the Deep South in the World Above.

Allure turned her head downward, placing it on Desiree's shoulder, as she pretended the world had just come to an end.

As Marbleman neared Desiree, the corner of her mouth turned upward, exposing her beautiful, perfect front teeth.

"Wow," said Marbleman involuntarily as he marveled at her brilliant smile.

She continued in her fake Southern drawl, "Since we don't see eye-to-eye on this fine evening, but I am sure we will someday, I want you to meet a friend of mine. He likes to help marble people see things my way. So, sweetheart, I need you to show me how to unlock and use this elegant freezing spar tonight, or I am afraid my friend will persuade you to show me."

An enormous marble rolled in between the sisters and Marbleman, then shifted into his human battle form. He stood several feet above Marbleman's head, with his freezing blade on fire.

"Holy buckets," flowed out of Marbleman's mouth. *That's the biggest marble I have ever seen. Well, next to Menacing Strong…*"

"This is my friend Intimidor," Desiree chuckled.

"Holy *buckets,*" repeated Marbleman, as a tether of wet leather whipped at him from Intimidor's other hand. Before he could say another word, or move, the tether wrapped around him, scrunching his whole body together.

It ain't over. I still have a freezing blade in my hand, thought Marbleman, as his brain began slugging out ideas to escape.

Laughing uncontrollably, the big marble pulled Marbleman, who was now helpless, close with the tether. In a low, deep voice, he said, "I am Intimidor."

"I bet that's all you can say, you big brute," replied Marbleman, defiantly.

Laughing even harder, he repeated, "I am Intimidor."

"Hold on, I am coming brother," yelled Ironstone, as he rushed forward, with Moss at his side.

"Son of a blade," swore Ironstone, as a new assault of a dozen enemies rolled out of the woods. The came out from all directions, cutting them off from his brother.

"Fight for your life," commanded Moss to Ironstone, as the two quickly began counter attacking those foes rolling into the campsite.

"What the heck?" said Marbleman, as he felt a slow burn of the freezing process, as if struck by a blade. *This is a freezing rope. It's slowing freezing me. I must get out now*, he thought.

With the last ounce of movement in his wrist, he rotated his freezing blade upward, cutting the freezing rope in half by his waist, breaking the freezing process. In an instant, he made a decisive freezing blow straight into Intimidor's gut.

"Oh my," Marbleman said, as he looked upward to Intimidor's eyes, which remained unchanged.

Intimidor smiled big again, and said, "I am Intimidor."

"You son of horse thief. Don't you freeze?" asked Marbleman, as he began an onslaught of probable freezing strikes all over the giant. Marbleman's quickness outmatched the giant's slow attempt to wrap the other half of the tether around him again. Likewise, he avoided being struck by the powerful home-run swinging attempts by Intimidor. On the next low, big swing by the colossal foe, Marbleman leaped upward, shifting into his round form and high jumping the swinging freezing blade. Before hitting the ground, Marbleman was back in his human form, landing right next to Desiree. "Thanks," he said, as he ripped his Spewing Spar out of her hand.

"Hey," she shouted right back, as she failed to hold onto the weapon.

Like a fresh breath of spring, the blade and its rightful owner, renewed their connection. The blade fired up, glowing with shimmering reds and blues, full of powerful crackling freezing power. Instantaneously, six bolts of freezing power blasted out the weapon, striking Intimidor high to low.

The streams of power flew back into the blade in Marbleman's hand, as all of time stood still for a moment.

"I am Intimidor," were the last, and again, the only words he said, as the swift freezing power overtook the giant.

What the heck, he is not returning to his round form when frozen. Wow, it sure is a strange world her in the outer ring, as I thought all marble people retuned to the natural form when frozen. He looks like a frozen mountain, capped with snow, thought Marbleman, as he tilted his head back and forth. He watched for a moment longer at the frozen monstrosity who stood before him, who did not return to marble form.

Rapidly, Marbleman turned his attention to the skirmish behind him.

Nice move, brother, he thought, as Ironstone worked in unison with the old agate's freezing strikes.

Ironstone shifted into his round form and shifted back again to strike those standing in between the multiple freezing bolts from the old agate's freezing Spewing Spar. The two friends were clearing the battlefield of enemies, when a third, fourth, and fifth wave of Red Rogues and Tyrannicals came charging out of the woods in full attack.

Marbleman quickly moved between the foes to stand next to his brother and Moss, as the evil ones encircled them. "This is becoming a bad habit brother, being encircled by bad guys," said Marbleman, as tapped his brother on the shoulder.

"I have seen worse," lied Ironstone.

"Marbleman, seek the Manifest Power of Peace. It is within you to control your weapon. Now concentrate," cried out Moss Agate.

Scrunching his whole face with concentration, Marbleman thought, *I do feel strong... I can do it. I feel the powers of energy around me. It is right to freeze in the name of protecting others from those evil-minded foes who follow the power of war. I do believe in the Manifestation of Peace. It is virtuous.*

To Marbleman's surprise, his spewing spar burst freezing flames straight up into the air, and then flung downward, forming a protective lasso around the three friends. It froze anyone who attempted to cross the freezing stream.

I got it. You, my weapon, are a highly-skilled fighting machine for virtuous intentions. That's your name, isn't it? Your name is Virtuoso, he silently communicated to his spewing spar.

"You got to be kidding me. Will this never end?" said Ironstone, as a sixth wave of dozens more enemies piled in behind the others.

"Corrosos," muttered Moss.

"What?" replied Marbleman, anxiously looking all around at the steady stream of enemies making their way out of the woods.

"Those large, bluish and reddish mixed colored marbles back there are Corrosioannsdeeps; just know as Corrosos. They're a pack full of the meanest, cruelest race; meaner than any Red Rogue or Tyrannical," explained Moss, quickly.

They must be relatives of the Intimidor giant guy. What the heck? They are huge, all of them. I can't fight an army of giants. I can't fight them all, Marbleman thought, making him lose his newly found convictions and concentration. The protective freezing lasso ring around his brave little group zipped back in to his weapon, leaving them wide open for attack by the horde of bad guys surrounding them.

"Get them. Attack now," came a command from a leader of the foes, as the sunrise peeked over the trees.

The brave three fought all night but readied their weapons again. They planted their feet into the soil, ready for another round of freezing sword fighting brought on by the overwhelming number of assaulting foes.

"Now what?" asked Marbleman, as thousands of voices came from the forest in a repeated high-pitch battle cry of, "Ya, ya, ya, heee."

"Like there are not enough evil ones to fight around here. More are coming? How strong do they think we are anyway?" questioned a weary Ironstone.

The horde of attackers turned to look at the woods behind them, as Moss triumphantly blurted out, "Those are not more bad guys. Those are my friends, and they have answered my plea for help. Cattail Claws and her clan of women are here."

"The who?" said Marbleman, as the first of the women warriors burst out of the shadows of the thicket with such a powerful leap, she rotated head over heels in the air, while shooting off at least three freezing arrows. Each hit their marks, freezing the enemy instantaneously, before she landed, planting her two strong legs right next to him in the inner circle. "Holy smokes, freezing arrows?" blurted out Marbleman when she landed.

Wow she is beautifully muscular and rather large. Why, she probably could take me with one arm tied behind her back, were the thoughts that jumped into his head.

"It's about time Cattail," cheered Moss.

"It looks like the right time to me," answered Cattail, as she let more of her arrows fly.

"Incoming," shouted Ironstone, as four more warrior women leaped as if they could fly, into the inner circle to help fight off the enemy.

As if on cue, the edge of the woods all round the campsite battlefield erupted with dozens and dozens of the Claws Clan women, each attacking with their freezing arrows, flying from every direction. Not even the big Corrosos body could resist freezation from the powerful freezing arrows.

Moss commanded to the brothers, "Now is our turn. Fight for our freedom. Just be one with your weapon Marbleman. Let the power flow from within."

"I do believe in the Power of Peace," Marbleman boldly said aloud for the first time in his life. "Virtuoso, let's roll." The weapon spewed out freezing fiery bolts left and right, crisscrossing with Moss' own Spewing Spar bolts. Each struck and froze dozens of foes at the same time.

"Look out, Carbine," warned Cattail, to one of women warriors in the circle, as an enormous Corroso broke into their defense line, with his freezing blade fixated on the woman.

"Not on my watch," retuned Ironstone, as just in time, he deflected the freezing blade from striking the Claw Clan woman standing next to him. With a sudden surge of chivalry, he muttered to himself, "I've got this." He leapt over the second blade swipe attempt by the Corroso, as he shifted into his round state in midair. He struck a freezing blow to the foe's head and landed back in his human battling form with both feet firmly on the ground.

"Great move, handsome," said the sturdily built warrior, as she slapped his back, nearly knocking him off his feet.

The battle quickly ended, as the Claw Clan women spread out, freezing or driving the enemy away.

"Warriors, gather the frozen, and hide them in our secret holding place, so they may never be unfrozen to terrorize this land again," commanded Cattail.

The women warriors busily rolled off the frozen into the woods.

"Come over here boys and I'll introduce you," said Moss. "This is your rescuer, Queen Cattail Claws. I believe you, Ironstone, have meet her kid sister, Princess Carbine Claws."

"So, you're Marbleman. Word has spread rapidly about you being the one to prevent Menacing Strong from taking over these lands, as many fear him," the Queen said, as she slowly walked in circumference around him, sizing him up. She stepped forward and flicked his long, dark hair.

"Thanks for your help. We were in quite a bind," said Marbleman.

"I have a feeling we are not done yet helping you out," said Cattail, turning to walk with Moss Agate, clearly wanting to discuss something away from the group.

"Well," said Ironstone, turning his attention to Carbine, "you all kind of look a bit like cats. Real cute cats."

To which she spunkily replied as she marched away, "And you all don't look like dumb imbecilics from a Hicksville village."

"Nice going brother. You're off to a smooth start with the Princess," jested Marbleman. "Why don't you tell her next time that she looks like a cow, too. See how that goes, ha, ha!"

"Those Cattail floozies are not for you, my Marbleman," said the forgotten Desiree over the now almost vacant battlefield as her sister shook her head up and down in agreement.

"What? Hey you're still here? How the heck did you not get frozen?" said Marbleman, with his brother at his side again, readying for a fight with the sisters.

"Marbleman, my sweetheart. My offer to go to Tir na nOg with you still stands. I will see you again toot sweet." With her sister at her side, the pair once again winked one eye each, while blowing air kisses to the brothers. Then they disappeared into the deep thicket.

Chapter 4
Granite Death Halls

"Now that the King has fallen to Menacing Strong, there is nobody to stop him from conquering the city of Marbleutopia and making all of Marble World fall under his oppressive rule," stated Cattail Claws, as she walked with Moss Agate on the edge of the campsite.

"There is one," said Moss.

"Do you really think that young boy, Marbleman, is he the next true blood heir to the throne? Even if he is the heir, Menacing will never give up the crown, Diamond Glory, once he has it in his tight fist. I am afraid Menacing has amassed such a large army that there is not much one boy could ever do to stop him. Not only that, but time is running out, as it will be soon that Menacing will have gathered his army at Marbleutopia for his attack," said Cattail.

Moss slid his right foot back and forth in the dirt as he aimlessly watched a swooshing mark develop with his foot before he spoke. "True, there is not much one boy can do, but all of us who believe in the Manifest Power of Peace can move mountains. That includes whatever mountain Menacing Strong sits on. At this time, the boy is only the spark to unite all. We need the King back with his Stainless Steel personal guards. Don't forget the King has many allies that are loyal to him as well. There are many nations in the burbs around the Capital City that will rise up to his call. And don't forget most importantly, the four generals of Marbleutopia have a most formidable fighting force."

"But everyone knows the four generals have many obligations that spread them throughout our World Below and the World Above. Why, who can even remember when they all were in one place at one time? It would take a miracle, a speedy miracle, to get word to them to get their armies together in time to protect Marbleutopia before Menacing Strong wages war on the city. Millions faithful to the King will be frozen forever," said Cattail, as she shook her head back and forth, while looking at Moss.

"Hope grows from the smallest of seeds. Will you join us?" asked Moss.

"Your romantic sense of hope is impossible. Yes, I and a hundred of my best warriors will help you on this no-win raid of the heaviest guarded fortress in all the lands. Tonight was so much fun. We haven't been in a skirmish for years, so I will not even count this as a favor. Consider it free. But his Granite Death Halls thing…you will owe me big time," said Cattail.

"Agreed," promptly replied Moss.

Marbleman and Ironstone caught up to Moss and Cattail on their walk.

Marbleman said, "Do you believe those two wild Sapphire sisters. They don't give up. Did you see they were still hanging around after the battle?"

"No, I did not see them. Is your weapon safe?" questioned Moss.

Marbleman smiled big while patting his Spewing Spar for Moss to see the weapon was secured at his side. "You know the saying fool me once, shame on you, fool me twice, shame on me. Those floozy sisters are not going to shame me again. They're never getting ahold of my Spewing Spar."

Looking at his feet Marbleman aimlessly kicked a small stone back forth with his foot when he announced, "By the way I named my weapon. I call him Virtuoso."

"You named your weapon? Isn't that kind of weird," said Ironstone.

Moss quickly interjected, turning to Marbleman, "Oh no, that is very good to name one's mystical weapon. A Spewing Spar is no ordinary weapon, either. Naming it is another step forward in melding your thoughts with its thoughts."

"Still weird," said Ironstone raising one eyebrow at his brother. Not being able to resist, Ironstone continued to poke fun at his brother, "I hope you two will be happily melded."

Moss quickly changed the subject by half joking around. He said to the brothers, "I think we could use a little company on the trail to Granite Death Halls, as Queen Cattail and her clan agreed to protect us from any evil marble trying to freeze your skin."

Cattail bowed, saying, "Besides those who want to freeze you with their swords, there are the flying beasts made of steel. Some say they're a cross between dragons and birds. Why, their enormous beaks are said to be able to crack marble shells in half. It is also said their feathers are made of titanium steel and their talons are so large they can scoop up several warriors at a time and haul them off to be frozen in Granite Death Halls. So, you do need protection, as I bet you two are no good at shooting dangerous beast made of steal out of the sky, are you?"

"You mean mythical flying steathbills? Everyone knows those aren't real. But again nothing makes much sense on this adventure, so why not? I bet you and your clan are expert bowwomen at shooting anything out of the sky," said Ironstone going with the flow of the ongoing new lessons of this strange world in the outer rim, far from his home.

Returning and joining the conversation, Carbine Claws said, "Wait and see for yourself. Even steel freezes from our arrows, Mr. Villager."

"In all seriousness, we need to get moving. We have far to roll yet and Menacing Strong's armies are moving closer to the city every day," said Cattail.

"Let's roll," commanded Marbleman, and the newly formed troop all shifted into their marble forms for a fast roll to the gates of Granite Death Halls.

After hours of rolling, Ironstone turned to his brother. "How does such an old agate roll so fast? And how does he know where we are going? It's like a jungle here and I don't see any path."

"I don't know, but just keep up. Keep him in sight. We don't want to get lost out here. Besides we can't let that old agate and these claw ladies out roll us," said Marbleman.

"Here it is," shouted Moss to the group, as they came upon the chutes that lead to Granite Death Halls. He shifted into human shape and stood on the middle chute out of ten. He turned, kicked some dirt off the chute and waited for all the clan to catch up before he spoke. "These ancient chutes can take us all the way to the main gates of the halls. However, we will only travel until the chutes run by the river. These chutes will subdivide into hundreds of chutes before Granite Death Halls in order to accommodate the thousands of Menacing's battling forces when they come and go. If luck is with us, we should not see any of his troops on the chutes, as most are on their way to attack Marbleutopia. At the river, Queen Cattail will take all of you clan women to hide in the woods outside of the gate to wait for us. Marbleman, Ironstone, and I will go to a seldom used gate where the river runs under beneath the halls. I hope with such a small number, we can sneak up to the halls, and once inside, quietly find the King and the others undetected."

Ironstone was pointing around with his finger to count the Cattail Clan women as they gathered. He said, "Ah ha, just as I thought, there are not a thousand clan women. Why, there are only a hundred to my count. Back at the campsite battle, it sounded like so many more."

Undetected to Ironstone, Carbine was standing next to him again, and she said, "We are great in making it appear that we are many. And just how many warriors who have trained their whole lives with freezing arrows did you bring?"

"Well, none, but…" Ironstone tried to finish.

"Well nothing. We brought a hundred warriors with thousands of handcrafted-to-perfection freezing arrows. A hundred is all we need," proclaimed Carbine.

"Okay, you two love birds cut it out," joked Marbleman. "We are all here to work as one. We must save the King and father," encouraged Marbleman.

"We must roll very quietly from now on. We need surprise on our side. Look at the fresh dirt on the chutes. There could more enemies around here. Be absolutely silent," demanded Moss.

After rolling silently for a long time, the group finally came to the point where the chutes met the river, overlooking desolate flat lands.

"Oh, my word," said Marbleman, shifting to his human self as his eyes tried to absorb the enormity of what he saw.

"Is that…is that the infamous Granite Death Halls?" asked Marbleman.

"Yes, I'm afraid so," replied Moss.

Ironstone stood next to his bother and said, "Holy buckets, that front wall must be over a mile long. You weren't kidding old agate. There must be hundreds or even more chutes running up to that fort wall. But you didn't tell us how creepy the place looks."

Not expecting an answer, Marbleman added, "Is everything black down there? All the trees are gone. Nothing moves. Is all life gone too?"

"Yah and what are those things flying over the halls? Are those beasts of steel that Cattail talked about? And what is with all that smoke coming out of there?" added Ironstone.

"My boys, get a grip on your nerves. Yes, it is a most scary place, full of evil. It offers no comfort, but we must be strong, as the King need us," said Moss, to calm his young companions.

The sight of Granite Death Halls sickens me. It is much worse than I ever imagined. Wow, look all the clan women aren't moving. I guess they're worried about what they see down there, too. Nobody is moving a muscle, thought Marbleman. *Is the air here chilly? I feel cold. Burr. It is getting colder? I can admit to myself that I am scared. I can see dozens of torches burning on the sentry posts. That dark ice is streaming down all over those walls. Those birds, no they look more like dragons flying around, just like the ones that were told in old fairy tales. They look like big time trouble.* He shook his head back and forth, feeling his eyes well up. *What have I gotten myself into? I have dragged my brother into this mess. What if he is frozen for all eternity? I will never forgive myself! What am I doing here anyway, I am not a warrior. I can sense a change in the Power of Peace. I can feel it. It is the Power of War. It is reaching out to me.*

Dark thoughts continued to race around in Marbleman's head when he heard a deep voice beside him, "You are on the wrong path of life. You can be the supreme leader overall, even over Menacing Strong. Choose the enlightenment of the Power of War. Join me."

"What the heck?" Marbleman turned quickly around, looking for the source of the voice, but no one was there. He rubbed at his eyes. "Great now I am losing my mind," he said to no one in particular.

"What did you say brother? Is something wrong?" asked Ironstone.

"I guess not, " replied Marbleman.

"Snap out of it. Stop staring. We've got a job to do and we are going down there to save the King and the rest. I know it is overwhelming when you first see Granite Death Halls, I should have prepare you more, but we must get moving," Moss said, as he grabbed an arm of each brother, yanking them off the trail of chutes, so they could take the one to the river. Come now. We must follow the river quickly before we are seen. Follow me," he directed.

Without a word Queen Cattail and her clanswomen followed the plan. They climbed off the chutes in the other direction, heading deep into the woods before any guards on the walls of the fortress in the valley below could see them.

"Oh my," said Carbine, as she continued looking at the enormous walls of Granite Deaths Halls. She was the last to climb off, but she looked back and caught Ironstone's worried eyes watching her. Then Moss yanked the brothers off the chutes, putting them on the path of the river in order to find their king.

Chapter 5
Dungeons of Granite Death Halls

"We're almost there. Wait a minute can you hear it? A stealthbill is coming. Quick, hide. Get on the ground now," commanded Moss Agate.

Marbleman and Ironstone hunkered down under a small shrub that was trying to make a come back in growth. The steady beating sound of the creature's deep and powerful wing strokes in flight sent a chill through both brothers.

As the beast passed overhead, Marbleman thought, *I wonder how many of the Cattail's freezing arrows would be needed to bring down such a big bird? Or could they really freeze such a beast of the air? Geez, I am glad it didn't see us. Sure is a scary creature.*

"That was way too close," said Ironstone as the beast disappeared from their sight, passing over the great wall that stood before them.

"We made it this far, unseen even under the watchful eyes of Menacing Strong's beasts of steel flying in the sky. This strip of small struggling trees and bushes along the river hid us well. There, see? There is the old waterside gate," said Moss Agate, pointing. "The river is not deep right here. I know, as I used to wade around here in the river when I was a young apprentice. I used it for morning contemplation of the Power of Peace. But I must warn you that not far inside the wall, the river turns very powerful, sweeping everything into the muddy abyss deep beneath the fortress. There are far worse things down there than mud and water. Nobody who has been taken away by its strength has ever returned," warned the old agate.

Ironstone looked at the water flowing through the metal gate and said, "Oh no, more water. I don't swim so well. Actually, I don't think I can swim at all. I am really learning to hate rivers."

Following Moss, Marbleman stepped into the shallow river, pulling half dead vines off the front of gate and surrounding wall.

Clearing the entrance, Marbleman said, "Great, we found it, but how do we get pass it? That gate looks like it hasn't been opened for years and it also looks well fortified. It looks like there is not just one gate, either. It looks like there are two gates, both made of heavy iron."

"We certainly can't go over the top of the wall. How tall is it anyway? One hundred to two hundred feet of solid black granite? And look at that--it looks like it slants outward. Nobody but a spider could climb that kind of a reverse slant of a wall," said Ironstone, stating the obvious.

Reaching for the thick, tarnished old chain around his neck, Moss produced two large rusty, old-looking keys.

"This should do the trick," he said.

Just one inch from inserting the key, Moss hesitated, and then turned back to talk to the brothers, as Ironstone joined them in the river. "There used to be a guard post on the other side. I am hoping the post has been abandoned, since nobody comes this way anymore. If there is still a guard on the other side, there is little chance of us getting by without being seen. If the main old grumpy guard is still at the post, I don't think he will be pleased to see me. He is one of the meanest of Menacing guards, and frankly, the dumbest. He is known for his doubletalk and nonsense. He would sell his own mother for a price, as he is both a fool and easily swayed. But he should not be trusted. If we run into him, I'll deal with him. Yes, looks like my key still fits," said Moss, as the rusty first key turned in the equally rusted keyhole.

"Come on, push harder. We got to move this gate," called out Marbleman.

The gate let out a high-pitched squeaking sound that rose above the babbling of the river.

"Oh no…that noise is loud enough to wake up the all the guards in the whole fortress," said Ironstone.

"Hurry, let's get through the second gate before someone alerts all the guards of our arrival," said Moss, as he unlocked the second gate.

All three pushed the gate open enough for them to squeeze through one at time, but it still squealed just the same.

"Holy cows, this gate is louder than the first," mumbled Marbleman.

"We are inside. Quickly, get out of the water and follow me to the…" Moss abruptly stopped talking. Seemingly out of mid-air, a huge guard, plus six other guards, stepped right in front of them.

"Just where are they going to follow you? You old, nasty wizard, Moss Agate," said the huge guard, with his freezing blade ready for fighting.

"Gobbledygook, it's so good to see you are still the main guard of this gate. I hoped to see you. It has been many years. How are you and the little missus doing?" said Moss, cleverly.

"First of all, I don't have no little missus. And second, you left me frozen the last time I saw you. In fact, it was when you escaped right here on this very spot. I never thought I see you return unfrozen. So I am going to freeze…" Gobbledygook was cut off, as Moss already sent six freezing bolts from his Spewing Spar, striking the guard all over his body.

"Not again, you son of a horse thief," were the last words Gobbledygook managed to get out before he froze solid and reverted into his marble form.

Moss and his Spewing Spar were in full battling freezing mode. "Back with you to your dark corners," he shouted at the other guards, as his Spewing Spar sent one freezing bolt in every direction. Each hit their mark, freezing all of the guards standing behind Gobbledygook.

The brothers rushed beside the old agate, but they were too late to help, as Moss Agate single-handedly froze all the marbles guarding the gate.

Moss turned to the brothers, "Hurry, we do not have much time, as another patrol of marbles will likely be coming soon. When they do, they will see all of the frozen bodies and sound the alarm for the squadrons to come."

"Too late. The alarm has been already been sounded," came a deep voice from the shadows.

"Oh no, it's Curmudgeon," said Moss to the brothers quietly.

"Curmu----who?" said Ironstone.

Moss whispered, "Curmudgeon. He is the Overseer Commander of all of Granite Death Halls. He is the meanest of the mean. This is not good, not good at all."

"Geez, how come his freezing blade looks two times bigger than anybody else's?" commented Ironstone, as he took three steps backward.

"Because it is," said Moss matter-of-factly.

Moss' eyes narrowed, as he tightened his lips and spread his feet, planting his rear foot firmly in the ground. With his weapon raised for battle, Moss gave Curmudgeon his full, serious attention.

"Curmudgeon," acknowledged Moss, giving Curmudgeon a nod.

"Moss, you old scum of a traitor. It has been a long time," Curmudgeon said, as his freezing blade pulsed from blue to black freezing flames, as he advanced toward Moss.

Moss motioned to Marbleman and Ironstone to stay back.

"Look out," yelled Marbleman, as Curmudgeon took a full-out swing at Moss with his freezing blade.

Moss ducked just in time, as the freezing flame from the blade zipped past his head. But with a well-rehearsed second swing, the flame caught Moss in his right thigh.

"Oh no," cried out Marbleman, as he could see the freezing process of blue coloration creeping up and down on Moss' body from the strike point.

"You old betrayer. You have become a rusty old wizard. Let me cut your legs off by the roots and put an end to your treachery," laughed Curmudgeon.

Virtuoso's power rose, glowing stronger and brighter as the freezing flames flickered from left to right. Narrowing his eyes on Curmudgeon, Marbleman challenged, "That cuts it…come here you skunk. We're not so rusty."

"My pleasure, young marblerats," gleefully responded Curmudgeon.

"Come on brother. We have got to help the old agate. Go left," yelled out Marbleman to Ironstone, who quickly moved to the left side of the nasty guard.

Marbleman went right, so the three of them together made a triangle fighting formation around Curmudgeon.

Moss pulled out his leather satchel and sprinkled a purple colored dust all over his body, which slowed and then began reversing the freezing process.

"Nice," called out Marbleman to Moss, for yet another clever mastermind trick.

"I see, you have a Spewing Spar, too. You must be the one all the fuss is about," Curmudgeon said, as he eyed Marbleman.

"Let's roll, you big lummox," challenged Marbleman, as Virtuoso fired a bolt of freezing power straight at Curmudgeon, who blocked the attack with his huge blade.

"Ah ha," said Moss, as he took advantage of the fact Curmudgeon was focusing on Marbleman. Moss released one straight and powerful freezing stream, hitting its target in the rear shoulder.

"Why, you dirty son of a cheapskate cheater. You'd strike one in the back?" protested Curmudgeon, as he began to freeze from the thunderous blast.

"You got to be kidding me," proclaim Ironstone, as Curmudgeon's body strength held off the freezing like no marble had ever done before. "Look out he is shaking off the freeze."

As Curmudgeon shook his body free of the freezing process, ice shards flew in every direction, with a big piece hitting Marbleman in the face.

"Ouch," said Marbleman, as Virtuosos responded with six freezing bolts of its own, striking Curmudgeon in separate points all over his enormous human form.

"You're flirting with disaster, young marblerat. I'll be back," were the last words Curmudgeon said, before his body gave in, shifting back into his natural marble form, completely frozen.

Chapter 6
The Dark and Damp

Moss nodded his head in approval. "Nice job. There are not many who can say they froze Curmudgeon and lived to talk about it. We must hurry. Curmudgeon may very well have sounded the alarm for other squadrons of guards to respond. There could be an army heading our way right now. Remember, inside the halls there are many more guards, traps, and nasty creatures. They're all laid out in a damp, dark labyrinth. Beware that the halls, at times, will only big enough for us to pass through in our natural marble being and at other times the halls will be big enough that we will be able to transform into human battle form. There are many places they may have hidden our frozen King and Gemstone. Follow me, we must begin our search now."

The three moved past the frozen guards at their feet. Just for a moment, Marbleman paused and marveled at the huge size of Curmudgeon, even in his frozen state.

As he passed, he tapped Curmudgeon on top, whispering, "Sorry about that. I didn't mean to freeze you so hard."

Swiftly, the trio walked to an inner granite wall with one doorway. Moss pushed the round, old, solid oak door open, relieved to see nothing but a pitch-black hallway.

Marbleman's head were a flurry of racing thoughts and doubts. *Here we go. I can't believe I am going into the infamous halls of Granite Death Halls. Yep, I remember as kid how scared I would become after listening to bedtime tales of this place. Oh well, it's not so bad. Wait, who am I kidding, it's awful. It stinks like frozen death. I think I've changed my mind; I don't want to go in there. Boy would I like to be back in my warm and safe bed in the village right now. Wait, I at least can see one faint light, way down there in the darkness. Thank goodness there are some torch lights.*

"Well brother, are you going to just stand there like a frozen statue? Or are we going to follow that old agate into the dark? Are you sure this is the right thing to do?" questioned Ironstone, as he placed one hand onto his brother's shoulder.

Marbleman's eyes softened as he turned to his brother. "Of course, I am not sure. Have you ever seen such a scary looking dark tunnel? But going forward is our only way, brother. Our father needs us."

All three marbles transformed into their marble form to pass through the round doorway, one at a time, to face the cold and damp.

It seemed like they were rolling forever, still not quite reaching the only torch light they could see, when Ironstone said, "That cuts it…there is cold water all over the floor. Why is there so much water around here?"

"I know I am rolling in it, too. It seems to be getting deeper on the floor. Look at the walls, water is dripping down the walls and forming ice too," said Marbleman, as his brother slowly rolled by him.

"But the old agate is still pushing forward. If he gets too far ahead, well never find him in this dark place. Besides, the floor is wet or icy…not good for catching up to him," countered Ironstone.

"Slow up old agate. It's not easy moving in this wet, icy, dark place and I think the water is getting deeper. We can barely see you," called out Marbleman.

"Come on boys. Keep up. I am sure by now the other guards have found the others and they will be coming after us. Keep moving," commanded Moss.

"Oh, here it is. We have made it to the Chamber of Halls. These passages lead to the dungeons where the frozen are kept. They are usually well-guarded, so they cannot be unfrozen to return to their life. Let's shift into battle form, as there are many guards lurking about in these halls, guarding the frozen. I suspect the frozen remains of the King and Gemstone are near," Moss called back to the brothers.

Ironstone was several feet ahead of his brother, with Moss entering the chamber, when he called out to Marbleman, "Hey brother, it's a big room. Kind of impressive."

"Ouch," Marbleman said, as he shifted too soon into his human self and his head hit the ceiling of the dark tunnel, just before the entrance of the chamber room.

"Look out, it's a trap," came a warning from his brother, who sounded very far away.

Marbleman flattened himself against the wall, looking into the darkness to find his brother. He heard nothing and he could see nothing.

What trap? I can't see either of them. Where did they go? he thought.

Marbleman gasped as his weapon glowed in its sheath, still attached to his leather belt. Pulling out Virtuoso to use as a torch, the chamber lit up as Marbleman wearily peered into the room.

"What the heck?" he said, stepping into the room, as the tall ceiling reached beyond his eyesight.

"Brother?" he said, only slightly louder than a whisper. Marbleman got no reply from any of the passageways.

Horse hockey. What happened to them? Where did they go? What kind of trap was it? I can't see any trap. Which way should I go? he thought.

Then he heard a voice coming from direction he just came.

"Brother is that you?" he said softly, but then realized it was not the voice of anyone he knew. *Guards are coming and sounds like a lot of them*, he thought to himself.

He heard the voice again and it was giving commands. "We must find those treacherous scum. You take half of the squad and go down there. The rest of you, come with me to the chamber."

"Gadzooks, what am I going to do? Lights out Virtuoso," he said to his weapon.

The chamber grew dark as his Spewing Spar's light extinguished.

He again talked to his weapon, "Well, this could be the beginning or the end, but let's go this way." He picked the doorway on his near right, then stood motionless a few steps in the passageway to watch and listen in the dark.

The many guards' freezing blades' lights danced all over the chamber walls as the lead guard commanded in a hissy voice, "Divide up. We'll take the middle halls first and then circle back through the outer halls until we find them. We outnumber them a hundred to one. Freeze them on sight. Don't fail me or I'll have all of your stinking carcasses thrown into the muddy abyss below, where no one returns."

Without hesitation they all disappeared into the middle six tunnels.

"Whew, that was a close call," Marbleman said to Virtuoso, who responded back with two small flashes of light. "So, you can understand me, can't you?"

To which he received two more flashes.

"Let get out of here. We've got to find my brother and the old agate. They would not have just left me. Something bad has happened to them. Now then, which way did they go? I have no idea where they went. Shall we go back to the chamber or perhaps just follow this dark and damp tunnel? Well, at least I can stand in this hall."

Suddenly, Marbleman could hear the faint sound of crying in the distance.

Marbleman held his breath, listening. "Sounds like a female crying. Do you hear it, Virtuoso? Should we go see if she needs help?" To which he received three fast flashes from Virtuoso. "Okay, okay, we will go see what the weeping is all about. Maybe she's seen Ironstone and Moss Agate."

Marbleman walked cautiously down the tunnel. Soon, he saw an open, large doorway, from where both the crying and dim light where coming from. He peered in the room.

"Oh," he said, as he startled a beautiful young female with wet, hot tears melting swatches of ice that was trying to overtake her body.

"Oh," she repeated. Her lips clamped shut and she nibbled softly on her lower lip.

Standing still, Marbleman locked his eyes hers. *Blam damsel anyway, she is the most beautiful female marble, made from the purest glass I have ever seen. Her beauty is not like those temptress sisters, Desiree and her sister Alluree, but rather, a wholesome and warm beauty. My heart is going to pop out of my chest just looking at her sweet face. She looks so fragile, sitting there in the middle of the room, with light dancing on her clear marble skin and light brown hair. Or is her hair reddish? What the heck? Only half of her is frozen. She is frozen form her waist down. How is that possible?*

She broke the silence and quickly said, "Hey, you're definitely no guard. Who are you? What are you doing here? Are you on that ugly Menacing Strong's side or what?"

Marbleman just stared at her as he thought, *Oh my gosh, I have seen her before. She is the girl from the weird vision I had at the pond by the barn. What was her name again? Oh yes, Fragile something.*

"Well, are you just going to stand there or are you going to help me?" questioned the frustrated half-frozen young female.

"Sorry," said Marbleman. "I just was thinking that…"

"You were just thinking what?" she demanded

"I think I have seen you before," he said, with his eyes to floor.

"Hey, now that you mention it, I think I have seen you somewhere before, too. Have you been to my village?" she said.

"I don't think so. I have mostly been in Glory Village my whole life," he replied.

"Nope, that's not my village," she said, placing her finger on her chin in deep in thought.

"Holly crap," she blurted out, "don't get any big ideas, but I think I saw you in my dream. Is your name is Marblethran?"

"Close, my name is Marbleman. Is your name Fragile?" he said.

"Very close. I am Fragilian Glass of the glass marble clan. How did you know my name?" she said.

"Don't you get any ideas either, but I think I saw you in a dream, too," sheepishly replied Marbleman.

Fragilian Glass raised her eyebrows in surprise and asked, "Do you believe in the Manifestation of the Power of Peace?"

"I am not a hundred percent sure, but I am really beginning to think there is something to this Power of Peace stuff," he replied.

"I believe. I think the Power of Peace is at work here to bring you to me. How else would we share the same dream of knowing each other? We are meant to find one another for, some purpose," she proclaimed.

"What purpose?" he questioned.

"I am not sure but here we are," she replied.

An awkward silence fell between them.

To break the awkwardness, Marbleman said, "Of course, I am not with Menacing Strong. Sure, I will help you, but how? You're half frozen. I have never seen any like this before. Just how did you end up like this anyway?"

Her eyebrows furrowed, as she clenched her jaw, then said, "Just a couple of days ago, that low-down stinking, fat, old root of all evil, Menacing Strong attacked our village with his Furious Forces. I told him directly to his hideous face that I was not afraid of him. He just smiled back, saying I would be afraid of him soon enough, and that he would give me plenty of time to think about what I said to him. He told me I needed to learn respect and my proper place. That's when he half froze me, calling me a feisty young wench. Imagine him calling me a wench. Worst of all, he laughed the whole time at me. I had just finished my coming of age challenge and the whole village was celebrating. We did not have any of our weapons with us because of the celebration. Had I had my freezing blade with me, I would have shown him a few things about freezing."

Marbleman added, "I just passed my challenge too." He reached down, trying to pick her up, frozen half and all. "Urgg, I can't move you."

She frowned. "Why are you here anyway? In Granite Death Halls…"

"I am here to rescue my father and the King," replied Marbleman.

"Wow, so it is true. How about that? The king and queen, back together after all these years," she said.

"What do you mean?" asked Marbleman.

She smiled big. "Well, I overheard that big lummox of a dumb guard call Gobbledygook, bragging to other guards that he finally had both the king and queen frozen down here and under his control. I didn't believe it, because I just saw the king riding through my village the other day looking for Menacing Strong and his army."

Marbleman stepped toward her and questioned, "You mean, it is true the queen has been a prisoner here in Granite Death Halls all these years?"

"I guess so?" she replied.

Marbleman said, "First things first, how do we get you out of here? Heck, how can I get all of you unfrozen?" He paced around her frozen statue-like shape. "How indeed…how, how, how?"

She hung her head, looking at the floor, and quietly spoke, "Looks like you didn't bring any Nanoites? Everyone know Nanoites are the only ones that can unfreeze the frozen. But you didn't bring any did you? Did you?"

"I never thought about it," said Marbleman, shyly.

Wow how stupid am I? he thought. *I rushed here to save both the frozen King, who is my true father, and the father that raised me, not to mention, many more…without any plan for unfreezing them. There are too many of them to hand roll out of here. And now I lost my brother and the old agate, too. What a fool I am. Here I am in the middle of Granite Death Halls and I cannot unfreeze anyone to get them out of here. That old agate sure didn't have a plan for unfreezing. He got me deep into this fix. How stupid I must look to her. Pretty stupid I guess.*

"Ouch, that hurt," Marbleman, blurted out, as Virtuoso sent a small shock of pain into his hip. "Hey what was that for?" He looked down at his belt where Virtuoso was holstered.

"You talk to your freezing blade?" she asked in bewilderment.

"Well of course not, that would be weird," he quickly responded, only to receive another jolt of pain to his hip. "Okay, I guess I do, but it's no ordinary blade. It is a Spewing Spar with special abilities that, well, only masterminds can use."

"Oh my," she responded, after a long pause. After another long pause she spoke, "Are you a bad wizard?"

"No of course not. I'm not any kind of wizard. I'm just kid who knows how to use this way cool weapon." Marbleman jumped, as Virtuoso started tingling and sent out rapid flashes of light. "Take it easy," he said to his blade, as he pulled it from the sheath. "Whoa, that's a new color…*purple.*"

Fragilian's eyes widened, and her mouth fell open. "It's beautiful. I have never seen anything like it. Those red bursts are making the prettiest shimmering purple color I have ever seen."

Marbleman looked to his blade, whispering to it, "What are you trying to tell me? I got a feeling you're telling me we can unfreezing the frozen, but that's ridiculous…"

To which Virtouso flashed intensely, ready for the task.

Why, that the old mastermind agate knew I could unfreeze others with this Spewing Spar. He did have a plan. He is a tricky one. But now, how does it work? Could I hurt her? What if I freeze her to death? I don't know about this, he thought.

"Fragilian, I think I can unfreeze you with my Spewing Spar, but I am not sure. I have never done anything like that before. By the way its name is Virtuoso," said Marbleman.

Giggling, Fragilian said, "It's a pleasure to meet you, Virtuoso."

She was rewarded with three fast, bright flashes from Virtuoso.

"Well, I am not staying here. Just do it. Unfreeze me. I believe you and that magical talking blade can do it. I am not afraid. Anything is better than staying like this for the rest of my life. Please, just do it," she announced with determination

"What if I hurts when--" he tried to finish but she interrupted him.

"Go ahead do it, Marbleman. I am ready," she urged.

Without further thinking, Marbleman gently touched her with Virtuoso's purple flame but the contact was anything but gentle. Thunderous sounds and bright light flashed, sending a power surge right down his arm. It shot him backward and flattened him on the ground.

"Whoa, are you alright?" he shouted, even before his eyes cleared from the blast.

As his eyes cleared, Fragilian was already standing over him, as she reached her hand out to pull him off the dungeon floor. "You are quite the Marbleman. Look, I can still walk after being frozen. You did it," she said, as she embraced him with all her might, squeezing the living stuffing right out of him.

"Hurry, this way," came a distant voice, followed by many other grunting sounds and footsteps.

"Oh, we are in trouble now. All that unfreezing noise has brought the guards right to us," said Marbleman.

Chapter 7
Surprise in the Hall

"Let's get out of here before those guards arrive. It sounds like they are coming from that way, so I guess we better go the other way. Hurry Marbleman," said Fragilian Glass, pointing south down the hallway to the left.

"Darn right, let's roll," Marbleman replied, as both shifted into their fast rolling forms.

They barely started down the tunnel when they heard a guard behind them shout, "She's gone. The sassy young one is gone. Gobbledygook is going to freeze all our stinking marble hides for sure, if we don't find her."

Giggling, Fragilian said softly, "That Gobbledygook has a few more surprises coming his way because when I see him again, I'm going freeze *his* stinking marble hide."

"We better keep rolling," said Marbleman, as Virtuoso shot out a dim light for them to see thru the darkness.

"Hey, you can wield Virtuoso even while you're in rolling form, that's different," said Fragilian.

Marbleman replied, "Ya, everything seems different lately."

"Does it feel to you like we're rolling down hill?" asked Fragilian.

"I think so, but it does seem like we are going deeper and deeper into this place. I am not sure where we are at all. There have been so many turns and we have gone so far. I am afraid we may never find our way back out," said Marbleman, as he slowed his roll down, shifting into his human self.

Turning around, Fragilian also shifted, to face him as she said, "Hey, we can do this. We can find the King and Queen. I really believe that destiny has brought us together. We are meant to here and now to help others. Besides, who else is going to help them?"

"I know you're right, as I feel the same way, too," answered Marbleman.

"Wait just a minute. Listen. Can you hear that?"

"Hear what?" he replied.

"Douse your light. I am sure I heard guard voices ahead. Shush now and follow me," she said, as she used her hand on the icy wall to guide her balance, as she crept forward to the voices.

She put out her left hand indicating for Marbleman to stop. "Look there is a bright light down the hall and it looks like a lot of guard movement. There must be someone very important locked up on the other side of that dungeon door to have all those guards around," whispered Fragilian.

"Or maybe it is my father? Or maybe my brother or my old agate friend?" whispered Marbleman in return.

"What? Is your whole family down here?" she questioned.

"Pretty much. It's a long story but we need to find them all before I can leave here. I hope they all are behind that door," answered Marbleman.

"Let's find out. We can take out those guards together," she said with all confidence.

Marbleman turned his head and scratching his neck, he whispered, "Umm, you have no sword."

"Well, your fancy pants blade there can freeze a couple of those guards right away and with any luck I can nab one of their swords before they freeze. Then I can fight. Actually, I prefer two freezing blades, if you can manage that?"

"Sure, sure… Two custom, made-to-order freezing blades for the two-fisted little, fragile lady coming right up," said Marbleman, as he rolled his eyes up to the celling, then stepped in front of her to go on the offensive.

As luck would have it, two unaware guards strolled right toward them. Unseen in the darkness, they came almost nose-to-nose with Marbleman.

"Now Virtuoso," commanded Marbleman, and Virtuoso let out two quick pulses of freezing strikes, one for each guard. In a flash before the guards could even mutter a word, Fragilian nabbed each guard's freezing blade right out of their hands before they were sent into frozen oblivion.

"Hey, what was that?" shouted one guard from down the hallway.

Four of the guards swiftly advanced, two abreast in the narrow tunnel.

Nimbly, Fragilian charged the guards by running toward them and then sliding to her knees on the icy wet floor. She simultaneously froze both at their knees with her two-fisted freezing blades.

A long, "yaaaa-ha," was her high pitch battle cry, as she repeated the same trick on the next two.

"Wait for me—I'm coming," said Marbleman, running to catch up with Fragilian's aggressive attack on the guards.

"What the heck?" said Marbleman to himself, as he watched Fragilian advance her attack by running up the wall and summersaulting herself into the middle of the remaining guards, right in front of the dungeon door. She went up, down, turned, and circled, with both freezing blades going in all directions, seemingly at the same time. Within just moments, she single-handedly froze all the guards.

"Fragile, my sweet patooties," said Marbleman, batting his eyelashes.

"So, you like that, did you?" grinned Fragilian, brushing her long hair back in place, while revealing all of her brilliant, clear glass teeth.

"Now, if you could be a dear and just open this door with that magical blade of yours?" she playfully cooed at him.

Bowing to her, as if pleasing a crowed, he stepped over several of the frozen guards and rolled the last one away from the dungeon's solid oak door with his foot.

Even though she was right behind him, Marbleman still whispered in confidence to Virtuoso, "You can open this right?"

Reaching out to touch the door with Virtuoso, all of the door's brown color began turning, from the point of touch outward, into a frozen blue color. Then the door exploded into a million pieces from being frozen.

Marbleman smiled back in accomplishment, revealing his own dazzling white teeth as he said, "As you wish."

"Wow, it's a Fabulous Sphere," she proclaimed, as she entered the well-lit dungeon room.

"A what?" asked Marbleman?

Placing her hands on her hips and scrunching her face, she said, "Didn't your mother every tell you about the facts of the Queen. Everybody knows that, if and when, a queen is frozen they are encased in a *Fabulous Sphere*. I mean just take a look at it? The name speaks for itself."

Marbleman tilted his head left and to the right to take in all the beauty of the ornamental frozen sphere. The sphere was translucent, with a light ruby red color. Raised interlacing patterns of ice formed intricate geometric shapes across its surface.

"Just look at the changing colors of red and purple glistening off that sphere. I have never seen anything like this before," he said.

"Of course, you haven't ever seen it before. Nobody has seen a frozen queen. How do you know nothing about queens? Did your mother raise you in a barn or something?" continued Fragilian, shaking her head in disgust.

Marbleman responded, "Actually, I never had a mother, if you must know. Furthermore…" he stopped, as he saw a figure move inside the translucent sphere. Then it hit him, and he blurted out, "Holy moly, this *is* my mom."

"What in the blue blazes do you mean it's your mom?" Fragilian asked.

"I think that's my mother is in there," he said softly.

Fragilian tilted her head, raising one side of her cheek bones looking at him. Then she patted his shoulder and said, "Now, now there… I know it has been a tough day with everything going on and you think your whole family is down here, but this is the queen. Besides, you just said you don't have a mother."

Feeling like it wasn't the time to explain, Marbleman pointed to the sphere and said, "Look, is she sewing something on her lap?"

"I think so. It looks like a fancy doily," replied Fragilian, squinting into the sphere and trying to get a good look.

She tapped the sphere and the queen jumped inside, looking all around her surroundings.

"I don't think she can hear or see us. We need to get her out of there," said Fragilian. "Marbleman, you must do something. Please, unfreeze her right now."

Without a further word, Marbleman raised Virtuoso, whose flame was now a color that matched the frozen sphere of ruby red and purple tones. Then the spar touched the outer edge, there was no thunderous clash, but instead a hot gentle sizzling sound that slowly moved this way and that, making its way over the intricate geometric pattern as it melted the sphere away.

Time stood still, as out of the dissipating haze stood the queen. She was dressed in full brilliant white royal garments, with a flowing cloak, which offset her dazzling ruby red skin that was intermixed with wisps of pure white.

"Hey, her red and white skin colors look like your skin. If she had that sweet chocolate brown mixed in, you guys would be a perfect match," stated Fragilian.

The queen raised her arm and with an open finger, motioned for Marbleman to come closer to her.

"Me?" questioned Marbleman, as he looked over at Fragilian, who gave him a gentle shove forward.

The queen slowly ran her hand along his face, first his left side and then the right side. The room became even brighter with her smile, as one happy tear ran from her eye and she sweetly said, "I know that face. I have dreamed of that face. Even after all these years, I never gave up faith that I would see you again. I knew the Manifestation of Peace would bring you back to me, my son. Marbleman, I have missed you so."

"Mom," choked out Marbleman, as tears ran from his eyes and he embraced his mother for the first time in his life.

Fragilian wiped a tear from her eye, biting her lip as her go-to defense to prevent her from becoming swept over with emotions. "I am so, so sorry to break up this moment, but we really have to keep moving."

"Please forgive me son. We, your father and I, had to send you away for your own protection," said the queen.

"I know Mom, I know. There is so much to tell you, but not now, we should get out of here," said Marbleman.

Tilting her head to the right and downward, the queen looked over at Fragilian. "And just who is this? Your girlfriend?" inquired the Queen.

"Oh no, I mean no. Well, we just met and…" stuttered Marbleman, who was once again cut off by Fragilian's quick response.

"You would be so lucky to have me as girlfriend," she said, nudging him and nearly pushing him off balance. As he regained his composure, Fragilian then winked at him and laughed. "I'll have to think you over."

"I see," said the queen, smiling and tilting her head. She gently rubbed her chin, suspecting something was going on between the two of them.

Reaching her hand out to formally greet the queen Fragilian said, "My queen, my name is Fragilian Glass, of the Glass clan from Commonrock Village, and I too believe the Power of Peace is at work here. Now, let's go find your husband."

"What? My husband? You mean the king is here, too?" the queen questioned with excitement. Elegantly, the queen quickly calmed and said, "Oh my, where are my manners? I forgot to formally introduce myself. I am Ruby Tureround, Queen of Marbleutopia, and all of Marble World."

"Yes, your highness, I know. And yes, your husband is here somewhere," replied Fragilian, as the queen attempted to step forward. However, she fell from weak legs after being frozen for so long.

"I got ya. Nobody falls on my watch," said Marbleman, as both he and Fragilian grabbed one arm to steady the queen before she fell.

All three of them jumped when a voice rang out loud and clear at the doorway of the dungeon. "Ha, Ha… I almost forgot how beautiful you are my queen," said Gobbledygook sarcastically, as he blocked the exit with his freezing blade, ready for a fight.

Chapter 8
Where is the King?

"Gobbledygook, you dirty, fat old cow," screamed Fragilian, as she raced toward him, leaping in the air and summersaulting over his head. She landed softly and planted her feet firmly on the ground behind him.

As he turned around, she struck Gobbledygook, across his chest with one freezing blade, while simultaneously striking him low, across his knees, with her other blade, in a scissors type movement.

"Ughhhhhhh, not again… and frozen by a girl," whined, Gobbledygook, as the freezing rapidly flowed through his body and turned him back into his frozen marble form.

"I am not a girl. I am a lady," defiantly replied Fragilian.

"Humph." Gurgling was last sound from Gobbledygook, before his final frozen moment.

"What are you doing?" Fragilian shouted at Marbleman, when as she saw him sending a freezing blast right at her. She only had time to close her eyes when the freezing wave subdivided into five separate streams right in front of her face, each zooming around her. Mixed with the thunderous clashing noise of freezing, she heard the five guards behind her crying out in freezing pain.

"Oh, I see. Thanks," Fragilian said, as she walked back to hook her arm in the queen's again so she could help her walk around frozen Gobbledygook, and the other guards.

"Now what?" inquired the Queen, who was fast building her strength to stand and walk on her own.

"Well, we must find the others. Since we've already been that way, I guess we should keep going the other way," said Marbleman.

"Agreed," said the queen and Fragilian at the same time. Both females narrowed their eyes while wrinkling their noses at each other.

"Pardon me," said the queen to Fragilian. "Oh, I have been away too long. After all, this is your rescue mission. You're in charge."

"Wait a minute. No one is in charge. We all are here to work together to save the others," interjected Marbleman, trying to save the peace.

Fragilian smiled and said, "Absolutely, let's go find the others." She reached out to help her queen start down the endless narrow, pitch-black tunnel.

"How about a little light, Virtuoso?" said Marbleman, as he led the way into the darkness.

The tunnel floor was slanted downward under there feet. They walked cautiously for prolonged periods of time, as they did not know what trouble could be around any of the bends in the passageway.

Just as the group began to round a corner, Marbleman stopped and whispered, "Douse your light, Virtuoso."

Fragilian came close to his ear to speak softly in the dark. "What's wrong?"

"Listen… I hear something. I think it's more guards," replied Marbleman.

"You're right," said the queen. "I can hear them too."

Creeping forward, each kept one hand on the wall to guide them for a better look, when Marbleman stopped, saying in a low tone, "Look, there are double the guards outside that cell than you had, Mom."

"Well, that could mean it's the king in there, with that many guards to make sure nobody can get to him. Unfortunately, there are too many guards, preventing us from getting to him," said the queen.

"I like a challenge," said Fragilian a little too loudly.

"Shush," said Marbleman. "We don't want lose our element of surprise. We can't go back, so we will have to fight."

"I can fight, too," said the Queen, whipping out a concealed freezing blade from under her cloak.

Marbleman's jaw dropped, as his eyebrows lifted. "What other surprises do you have under that cloak, my queen?"

Smiling broadly, she said, "Never underestimate your queen. She is, I mean I am, full of little surprises."

Marbleman quickly put out his hand to stop Fragilian, as she began stepping forward for a yet another charging attack. He bent in and whispered frantically, "Okay, little fragile girl, I already know your style of fighting. Jump in now, plan later. But there is a heap full of bad guards down that hall. We need a plan."

"Darn right we need a plan. You attack high and I'll attack low. My queen, you clean up the rest," she said, bursting past Marbleman for the attack.

"Oh boy, here we go again. Come on," commanded Marbleman.

The guards were so busy, they did not see the threesome advancing on them.

Marbleman commanded Virtuoso, "Burst out high." Virtuoso sent an ear-splitting freezing blast above the gang of guards. The freezing bolt hit the ceiling, dividing into a dozen of smaller freezing streams, all bouncing downward and striking multiple guards.

Looking upwards at the freezing bolts above their heads, the guards did not see Fragilian sliding on her knees on the wet, icy floor toward them until it was too late. Six enemies were quickly sent to their freezing forms. Popping to her feet in the middle of the remaining guards, she began her two-fisted assault.

Marbleman ran though the crowd of guards, joining Fragilian back-to-back fighting off all those that opposed them when he thought he heard her say, *"You go right and I'll go left."*

"What did you say?" shouted Marbleman to her.

"I didn't say anything," Fragilian replied.

"Yes, you did," shouted back Marbleman, over the din of the fight. "You said go right and I'll go left."

"Hey, I thought that. I didn't open my mouth," she said, as she turned her head, and scrunched her eyes at Marbleman.

Can you hear me?

Holy buckets, I can, replied Marbleman in his thoughts, as he continued to battle the guards.

Keep rotating left. There are only a few left to take care of on that side, thought Fragilian.

Got it.

The two swiftly moved, rotating left in unison, freezing the remaining guards. Twirling around, the two turned and faced each other.

"What was that?" said Fragilian, who tilted her head sideways, and slightly downward, never taking her eyes off of Marbleman.

Marbleman broke the moment of silence and said, "Looks like you're trying to say something to me, but I can't hear you in my head anymore. Whatever that was it is gone."

"Thank all that is good, it's gone. There is only room for one person in my head and that is me. How dare you get in my head," warned Fragilian, who was unnerved by being able to hear Marbleman's thoughts during the fight.

"I had nothing to do with it. I was weirded out as much as you," he said, defending himself.

"Oh no, you don't."

Turning back to the direction they had come, the two of them saw the Queen make a mighty swing with her freezing sword, swiping a guard right across his forehead. He looked as though he thought he could manage to sneak away from the fight.

"Nasty mean old queen," were the words sputtered out by the guard, as he froze into his marble form.

All three rolled the frozen out of their way so they could reach the dungeon door.

Fragilian said, "Go ahead, Marbleman. Use that fancy freezing blade friend of yours and blast this door down. We need to get in there fast before more guards arrive."

"Okay, Virtuoso. You heard the fragile little girl. Do your thing," requested Marbleman.

"Wait," said the Queen. "Look here; it looks open," she said, pushing the dungeon door wide.

In the middle of the dimly lit room, with his back to them, stood a tall figure with a crown on his head. He also had on a royal purple robe, outlined in gold lace that draped all the way down his back and onto the floor.

"My King?" asked the queen warily, as the figure turned toward her.

"It is about time you recognize me as your king," laughed an angry Curmudgeon, who had returned from the frozen, shedding himself of his royal false disguise.

"It is a trap," shouted Marbleman.

"Attack," commanded Curmudgeon, to his guards who now poured out of the twelve or more doors that outlined the room.

"Blam damsel," swore Fragilian, at the sight of overwhelming number of enemies unabatedly rushing at them.

"Back, get back," shouted Marbleman, as they hurried back out of the dungeon and into the hallway.

Marbleman seal the doorway, Fragilian thought.

Great idea. And stop your swearing, replied Marbleman in his thought back to her.

Virtuoso instantly sent two intense waves of power; one going right and one moving left, and each cutting away the granite above the doorway. They fell hard, collapsing the opening.

"Look out, my son," called the queen, as a half dozen guards snuck through the doorway, as it was collapsing.

Fragilian charged, shouting, "You low down dirty old snakes in the woodpile." Fighting hard, she froze five guards where they stood.

"Oh no, you don't," warned the queen to the last guard, as she blocked his freezing blow attempt on Marbleman, who was deep in concentration, trying to finish sealing the doorway.

"Holy horse hockey," shouted the guard, looking to his right and seeing Fragilian standing right next to him with a very unpleased look on her face. She struck him high and low, in her well-rehearsed freezing move.

"Thanks," said Marbleman, nodding to both his queen and Fragilian, as the last of the tumbling rock sealed the doorway.

Right through the pile of granite rubble, the three could hear Curmudgeon shouting in anger, "Those lucky sons of horse thieves. Everyone, circle back around the other way. I'll personally throw each and every one of you in the muddy abyss tonight never to be seen again, if you don't deliver those marblerats to me, *frozen*. But I want the queen delivered to me in-person, unfrozen. Now go. Don't just standing there. Go, go, go."

"You heard him. We got to get out of here before they figure out a way around. Let's roll," ordered Marbleman.

All three shifted into their rolling forms, with Marbleman leading the way. Virtuoso's light bounced off his rolling shape, like a shining moon in the night.

Rolling swiftly along for quite sometime, Fragilian was the first to speak again. "How far do these tunnels go anyway? Don't they ever end? This way and that way. What the heck were the builders on when they dug out these hallways anyway? I am sick of all this darkens and sounds of silence down here. I can't wait to get out of here to see the open skies and hear regular sounds again."

Marbleman stopped and shifted to his human self, as did the others when he addressed her, "Fragilian, just remember why we are here. We will rescue the others and then get out of here to see the skies again."

"I know. You're right," said Fragilian.

"Hey kids, can we rest for a minute? I still feel a little bit woozy from being frozen for long," interjected Queen Ruby.

"Sure, but not long. We don't want to give all those guards a chance to catch up to us," replied Marbleman.

The queen leaned against a semi-dry spot on the icy wall, while Marblman and Fragilian strolled forward a little bit to see if anything was down the hall.

"I've decided," said Fragilian.

"What?" said Marbleman.

"I have just decided," she replied.

"Okay? What have you decided?" he said, playing along.

"So, I have thought you over, and I have decided if you keep playing your cards right when we are out of here, I'll let you ask me out for date. As long as you stay out of my head," said a frisky Fragilian, while she walked her fingers from his elbow up to shoulder, then tweaked his noise.

"Hey, you little…" but he was cut off as the queen came up behind them.

She urgently warned, "They're coming. I can hear a hoard of Curmudgeon's guards nearly here. Quickly, let's go."

They started to run.

"Whoa," said Marbleman, as he tripped, falling face first into a watery hole right in the middle the tunnel floor grasping on the edge

"It's no time for a bath," said Fragilian, trying to pull him up, but she too slipped into the hole.

"Marbleman," said Queen Ruby. Her face was lit by a freezing sword from a rather large guard, who held her by the scruff of her neck, then forced her downward.

"Don't you two little love birds move, or Queen Ruby here will returned to her frozen dreams. Oh, I have a surprise for you two," chuckled the guard, as he reached over with his other hand, pulling a lever along the wall.

"Oh no," cried out Fragilian, as water gushed down on them from the ceiling and sides of the tunnel. Both were knocked off their feet and swept down a hole in the floor.

"Hang on," shouted Marbleman, as they both caught the edge of the hole with their hands. Their feet dangled into the hole beneath them.

"Enjoy your stay in the muddy abyss," roared the guard, watching the two struggling to hang on.

"Laugh at this," said Queen Ruby, as she broke free from his grip falling to the floor and lifting the nasty old guard grabbing and throwing him over her shoulder.

"Hey," the guard protested, falling and sliding toward the trap hole.

"Blam damsel," swore Marbleman, as the guard slid into the both of them, knocking them off their tenuous hold on the edge.

"On no, Marbleman," Ruby cried out, as she ran over to reach for him, but she was way too late. Marbleman, Fragilian, and the mean guard all disappeared into the hole, just as a heavy trap door flung down, sealing them inside.

"No, no, no, this can't be happening," said the queen, as she tried with all her might to move the trap door.

Water filled the hole again, and she heard more guards coming.

Now what? she thought, looking around the area still lit by the freezing blade the guard had dropped when she knocked him off his feet. *I see… that's where the monster of*

guard came from. There's a cubbyhole in the wall next to the lever. How the fat old guard ever fit in there; I'll never know…

Picking up the freezing blade, she quickly doused its light, as she squeezed into the cubbyhole. It was just in time, as the first wave of guards stormed by.

The lead guard broke out his roll, shifting and standing right in front of the cubbyhole, with his back to her. He waved the hoard onward. "Come on, you maggots. Roll faster. We must get to the king so those traitors can't unfreeze him. You imbecilics, take the ledge pathway to the right or you just might enjoy the rest of your life in the muddy abyss." he shouted, actually hoping one or two of the guards might fall in for his entertainment.

As the last of the multiple of dozens of guards rolled by, the commanding guard stood silently in front of her hiding place. He looked around, then swiped his foot back and forth over the footmarks in the wet slushy floor where the queen knocked the guard over.

"Hummm," he softly mumbled, rubbing his chin. Then he slowly shifted back into his natural form and rolled off.

Crawling out of her hiding spot Queen Ruby thought, *Those guards are going to the king. I must follow them. If I can free him, then he will find our son and the others.* She walked gingerly on the narrow ledge on the right to avoid the hole. Looking downward at the swirly water covering the very spot where her son and Fragilian fell in she said, "This is only the beginning my son. I know the Power of Peace is with us. We will be reunited again."

Chapter 9
Shuffle to the Generals

I wonder what Marbleman and Ironstone are doing right now. I bet they're having a big victory feast, while I am here constantly rolling at backbreaking speed, all by myself, to get head of Menacing Strong's Army, thought Shuffleboy, rolling hard and focusing on his duty to warn the generals at Marbleutopia.

"Hey, hey… What do we have here?" heard Shuffle as he rolled into an open meadow.

"Oh no. Scouts," slipped out of Shuffle's mouth, as he tried to reverse his roll, but it was too late. A dozen human form scouts quickly closed ranks all around him.

"Very good, little rugrat. You know we're scouts of the strongest army in all the World Beneath. Menacing Strong has been looking for you and your friends. Now, where are they?"

Shifting into his human self, Shuffle said, "I don't have any friends."

"Liar. There are no second chance here. Freeze him, boys," shouted Slum Gulliam, Corporal of the scouting party.

"Wait just a Nano second. I am not armed," pleaded Shuffle.

"Well, you should've armed yourself if you're going to be spying on my army," replied Slum.

"Okay, okay. I left my friends a few days ago at an old barn, so I have no idea where they are right now," answered Shuffle.

Leaning over going nose-to-nose with Shuffle, Slum said, "I am not talking about days ago, nor no stinking old barn. You were seen just this morning with those other two spying on us. Tell me where they are, you treacherous spy."

"We are right here," came a voice behind the scouts.

"What?" asked Slum Gulliam, turning just in time to duck the first freezing blow aimed right at his head. Scouts to his left and right were not so luckily, as they fell frozen. "Yikes," screamed Slum, as he shifted, rolling fast off to the west.

"Dispute O'Leary bothers? What are your doing here?" questioned Shuffle, standing with his mouth wide open.

"First of all, you're welcome that we saved you from getting your hide frozen for all of eternity. Second, we are probably doing the same thing you are, heading to Marbleutopia," said Azurite Dispute O'Leary.

"Actually, it is good to see you in these strange times," said Baryocalcite Dispute O' Leary.

Monzite Dispute O' Leary walked up close to Shuffle and added, "Yep, we haven't seen anyone from the village since Marbleman, Ironstone, and you won our coming of age test. We left Glory Village after that fight, to, well you might say to lick our wounds, and when we went back there, was nobody there, including our parents."

"Ya, then we found this huge army headed west, and we knew this wasn't good. We been laying low, following alongside the army through the woods, trying to get to Marbleutopia for some answers," added Baryocalcite.

"Well, I know what happened to everyone in the village. It was awful, as Menacing Strong and his Furious Forces froze everyone, including King Trueround, who tried to stopping them. And ya, thanks for rescuing me," said Shuffle.

Azurite looked around the open meadow, sitting on one of the frozen scouts. "Hey did Marbleman get frozen too?"

"Oh no, he and his brother headed for Granite Death Halls to rescue everyone that were hauled off to the dungeons," said Shuffle, proudly.

"Do you think our parents are there too?" asked Baryocalcite

"Maybe?" said Shuffle.

"Well that will be the last we ever see of them. Nobody ever returns from Granite Death Halls," commented Monzite, looking down at the grass.

"So, what are you doing out here, anyway," asked Azurite.

"I am headed for Marbleutopia, to warn them about this army coming to attack them. But the army is spreading out so far and wide, I can't seem to get ahead of them.

This deep forest isn't helping any. I am not making very good progress getting through all this heavy brush. In fact, this meadow is the first clearing I have seen."

"Well, it looks like fate has brought us together, so we might as well travel to the city together," consoled Azurite.

"It is not fate, it is the Manifest Power of Peace that has brought you together," said a female voice from the edge of the woods.

All four jumped, taking a step backward, as the Dispute O'Leary boys all lit their blades readying for an attack.

"I mean you no harm. In fact, Moss Agate has sent me to help you," she said stepping out of the woods into the meadow. Continuing, she said, "I am Crystal Spheres. Like Moss Agate, I have mystical powers that can help you."

"Who the heck is Moss Agate?" asked Azurite.

Shuffleboy quickly added, "He is a wizard, but he likes to be thought of as a mastermind. Anyway, he is good. He is helping Marbleman."

"Hmmm," said Azurite.

Crystal said, "I am here to help you because you four are destined to come together. Combining your talents, you will be an invincible force to be reckoned with. You all are special."

Interrupting, Azurite spoke, "Ya, our mother used to tell us we were special, too. But you can see where that has gotten us. Nowhere, really."

"I am not your mother and I most certainly don't say things that are not true. I am compelled to be here by the Manifest Power of Peace. Together, you four have special powers to uphold the peace and protect others from harm. I am here to guide you to embrace your talents," she said, as her crystal skin glowed and pulsated with a bright whiteness.

"You seem sincere and all, but we are all nobodies from a small village, so having special powers is nothing we know about," said Shuffleboy.

"Oh my," Crystal said, standing right up after unintentionally sitting on one of the frozen scouts. "But you do have inner strengths that the Power of Peace will help to release. Why, Shuffleboy, your inner self is embracing all that is good about marblekind in the World Below, as you pride yourself on standing up for all that is just."

"Well, I guess so," quietly said Shuffle.

Continuing Crystal said, "And you three Dispute O Leary's always act real tough on the outside, but inside, your love for nature and all of its animals runs through your spirits. Especially your passion, Azurite, as you have the courage of a lion. Baryocalcite, you have the strength of ox. And you Monzite you have the bold sprit of an eagle who triumph over the skies. These ideas represent your inner strengths. These are the strengths you must embrace to protect the peace in the entire World Below."

"Hey, this is all heavy horse hockey. Just how do you know all that about us?" challenged Azurite.

"Well, since you're already skeptical of me, I guess it won't hurt to add more for you not to believe. My special power is that I can see into the hearts of marble people and see the future, too, and your future is about to change right now," she said.

Slum Gulliam laughed. "I love to hear all of these bedtime stories about special powers, but right now, my special power is that I, and my friends here, are going to freeze all of your stinking carcasses" boasted the returned Slum Gulliam, with a legend of armed scouts pouring into the open meadow.

"Son of a dull blade, we are in big trouble. There are way too many of them. Let's roll out of here," shouted Azurite.

Turning around, Baryocalcite shouted, "That ain't going work. Look behind us. There are a dozen more. We are surrounded."

Backing up to form a small defensive circle the four friend backs bumped into to each other "Hey, don't shift into your round form we need to stay in our human battling shape" yelled Azurite to Shuffle.

"I can't control it, I am shifting, something is wrong," replied Shuffle looking down his body turning into something he never seen before.

"Don't fight it Shuffleboy, let it happen, go with it is the Power of Peace at work," cheered Crystal.

"Hey, brother what's happening to both of you," cried out Azurite seeing his brothers shifting into each other and then into him

"Oh my stars," shouted Shuffleboy seeing all three of the brothers shifting vapors swirling into his body.

"Yes, yes, yes, it's happening, embrace the Power of Peace as the four of you will become one. Your true inner strengths are binding together as one living great tetramorph," shouted Crystal with glee.

Slum Gilliam and all of his scout stood motionless witnessing the change "What the son of a horse thief is going on. Just what the Blam damsel is that thing," questioned Slum? The scout next to him dropped his mouth wide open shrugging his shoulders saying, "Who knows what that is, maybe some sort of lion, cow, bird thing from the World Above."

Holly smokes, this is way cool. I feel super strong. Look at me, are those powerful paws, I feel bullhorns on my head, and are those wings on my back, Shffleboy thought.

Then he heard Azurite inside his head, *Correction I guess those feet, horns, and wings belong to all of us.*

Slum felt the hairs on his back rising as he step backwards commanding his scouting party "It still has the face of that rugrat or is it a lions face? Whatever that inferno that thing is freeze it now."

Shocked and afraid the scout next to him said, "You want that thing frozen you do it yourself as he shifted into his round form disappearing in to the deep forest with half of the other scouts.

"Attack now you sniveling cowards," commanded corporal Slum.

The remaining scouts lit their blades taking three steps forward when the Great Tetramorph Shuffleboy let out a huge roar lifting into the air by his wings spinning around in circle sending out a purplish freezing stream from his throat freezing all that were sounding him. "Gadzooks, what did I just do," he said.

Correction again, it is what did we all just do, said Azurites voice in his head.

Baryocalcite voice chimed in, *That was way beyond fantastic.*

The flying wing thing was the coolest part, replied Monazite.

"Menacing Strong needs to hear about this thing," spoke Slum to nobody rolling away from his hiding place behind a big oak tree.

Shuffleboy could feel a change happening again without his control "Now what's happening" he said out loud.

Crystal still standing by their side, "Remember don't fight it, the Power of Peace will guide your during all your tetramorph shifting.

"Oh that smarts," yelled Azurite as all four companions morphed back into their human form stubbing to ground.

"Yahoo, that's not for everybody," shouted Shuffleboy standing and congratulating all the brothers with heartfelt hugs and backslapping.

"Uh-oh, can you hear that. Is that Menacing Strong's army marching chant?" said Azurite.

"Yes, it is, and they are getting closer to Marbleutopia. I foresee that nobody has gotten word to the city yet of Menacing coming attack," answered Crystal.

"I don't like that war chant, it just plain creepy," Azurite said listening to the chant:

"Oura-uff, Oura-uff, Oura-uff, YoeeeeU—Corso; Oura-uff, Oura-uff, Oura-uff, YoeeeeU—Corso; Oura-uff, Oura-uff, Oura-uff, YoeeeeU—Corso, Hora, Hora, Hora!"

Crystal announced to all three, "Your calling is clear, you must complete Shuffleboy's mission to warn everyone in Marbleutopia with all speed that Menacing Strong's wild hoard is fast approaching."

Chapter 10
Into the Abyss

"Grab my hand," yelled Marbleman to Fragilian, pulling her close as they fell seemly forever downward in the darkness. "Now, shift before we hit bottom."

Fragilian let out an, "Uff da," as she smacked into the wet, muddy bottom. Sinking she converted back to her human self and opened her eyes just a tad.

Hey it is true. I can see underwater. Sort of...it so mucky in here and I can breathe, too. Marbleman, where are you? she thought.

Fragilian I am right here. Look for Virtuoso's light, Marbleman answered in his mind, as he took several steps forward and reaching for her hand again.

Come on follow me. Let's get out of here, thought Fragilian.

Wait, how do you know which way to go? I can't see a thing. It's too mucky, even with Virtuoso trying to light a path for us, he replied back.

I don't know which way, but any way is better than being right here. Come on, let's go, conveyed Fragilian, pulling his hand.

They both dragged and pulled their feet with all their might to move, and only edged a little bit forward.

Son of a dull blade, I can barely move, thought Marbleman.

"Holy buckets," screamed Fragilian into the muddy waters, as she bumped nose-to-nose with the guard they fell with from the trap door.

"Help me. Get me out of here. We are never going to get out of here......no one ever returns form this muddy abyss," rambled the guard, as he lost his footing and stumbled backward, disappearing into the muddy darkness.

Marbleman bumped into another muddy figure to his left, who cried out, "Help me. I have been here forever. Help me get out of here." He grabbed for Marbleman.

"Hey, let go of me," shouted Marbleman, shoving the unknown set of hands off him.

"Gadzooks," yelled Fragilian, as yet another set of hands, follow by another, and another reached out to grab her. "Please help us. Free us from this muddy gave."

Come on, communicated Marbleman to her, as they moved in the only free direction available to them, away from the hands.

But the rocky wall in front of them stopped them.

"You got to be kidding me. Now what?" said Marbleman, as he and Fragilian turned their backs against the wall to face the countless shadowy figures in the mud who were slowly closing in on them.

"What the?" yelled Fragilian, as another set of strong hands grabbed her by shoulders, yanking her straight up the rocky wall and out of Marbleman's sight.

"Fragilian," cried out Marbleman, as he too, was yanked up the wall by another determined set of hands.

Falling to his knees, exhausted, on the tip of a boulder, Marbleman wiped mud from his face in order to see who pulled him out of the muddy water.

He heard a familiar voice say, "It's about time you joined the party, brother."

"Ironstone," Marbleman said, as his brother gave him a welcoming slap on the back.

"So good to see you, brother," laughed Ironstone. "I thought we might not see you again. Especially after the old agate and I fell through a trap door and landed here. Say, how come you didn't fall through, too? And who is this fine young lass you dropped in with?" questioned Ironstone, playfully.

"Fragilian—where is she?" asked Marbleman, panicking.

"I am right here. This nice old agate lifted me out of the mud," said Fragilian.

Rising up, Marbleman went to her, giving her a full embrace. Looking at Moss over her wet shoulder, Marbleman eyes softened as he gently tightened his lips together and fought off tears. "Thanks."

"No problem, my friend," replied Moss.

Ironstone watched his brother hug the new girl and lifted his eyebrows high. He glanced at Moss for a brief moment and then addressed the new lady as he said, "I see…so your name is Fragilian? Well, I am Ironstone Landroller, Marbleman's brother, and this one who pulled you out is Moss Agate, our friendly guide to Granite Death Halls, who somehow seemed to forget where the trapdoors are located."

Raising his voice Moss said, "I already told you hundreds times that changes have been made since I was last here. You think I wanted to end up down here in the mud?"

Quickly interrupting to prevent further arguing, Fragilian said, "Well, I am so glad to meet both of you. We have been looking all over those nasty tunnels for you."

"We?" said Ironstone.

"Yes, we—and get you mind out of the gutter," snapped Marbleman. "I found her as a prisoner, half frozen, and being cruelly treated by Gobbledygook. I couldn't leave her, so she decided to help me find you guys."

"I showed that fat old Gobbledygook by freezing his keister a good one," she said, tooting her own horn.

Moss now raised his eyebrows at the accomplishment and said, "Is that so?"

"Yep, it's true. She can really handle herself around a freezing blade or two," boasted Marbleman.

"Oh no, what happened to the Queen?" said Fragilian, suddenly worried.

"Not sure, but she seemed to be able to handle herself too. After all, she knocked that old guard off his feet. We'll find the queen again," said Marbleman.

"Yeah, but doing so, she knocked us both down the trap door," stated Fragilian

"Well, she didn't mean to do that, I am sure," replied Marbleman.

"You found Queen Ruby Trueround?" came a voice from an unnoticed source on the far side of the rock top.

Marbleman swirled around and shouted in glee "Father, you're here. You're not frozen."

"Yes, my son I am here. Thanks, at least, to Moss Agate for the unfreezing me," Gemstone said, as he rushed over Marbleman, giving him a warm, tight embrace.

Turning to look closer at Fragilian, he reached out to take her hand, and said, "Who did you say this pretty maiden was that you just happened to find in these hall of death?"

"I am Fragilian Glass, of the Glass Clan. It's a pleasure to meet you sir," she answered.

"As you probably guessed, I raised both these boys. I am their father, Gemstone Landroller," he replied, with a huge smile on his face.

"And who are those two?" asked Fragilian, pointing at two others who had been silent so far.

Moss looked over his shoulder and nodded. "Ah, yes. Meet the ones who pulled us out of muck, Alnico and Ferrite Magnificents. They're cousins. There aren't many left in their Magnificents Clan. They haven't been down her very long, but just like us, they don't intent to stay here for a lifetime. I think they will come in very handy in terms of helping us all get out of here."

"Hi," both cousins said in unison, giving everyone a brief wave. The movement revealed more of their matrix of gray to white skin, with flecks of metallic flakes on their palms of their hands.

"Hey, what gives?" said Fragilian, as she felt she was being pulled forward by an unseen force toward the cousins.

Marbleman grabbed her by the arm, tightly holding her back, as his eyes narrowed, lips grimaced, and he held his blade tight.

Alnico quickly spoke, "Our apologies. Sometimes we can't control it."

"Control what?" demanded Marbleman.

Ferrite continued, "See, our clan's name is what we can do. We can pull others together, like magnets that can pull metallic objects. Only, we can do it with living beings."

"Really?" said Marbleman, not taking an eye off them.

"Quite harmless, they are, I assure you. They will be of great help to us in our endeavors," again stated Moss Agate.

"Hmmmm," said Marbleman, turning away to look at his father.

"Okay father, I have few questions you need to answer right now," said Marbleman, promptly guiding his father back to the far side of the huge rock for some privacy.

Reaching the edge of the rock, Virtuoso's light radiated over the mucky waters, revealing muddy lumps of movement all over in the mud. This prompted Marbleman to ask, "Are those all our kind stuck in there?"

"I'm afraid so. Some of them have been here longer than they can remember," replied his father.

"Why don't they get out of the mud and climb up to the top of a boulder, like we are? After all, there must be at least a hundred boulders all around here that I can see," stated Marbleman.

"It can be safer in the muddy water, as there is another danger lurking here, far worse that being stuck in the mire," said Gemstone.

"What danger? There's something lurking around down here?" asked Marbleman, now worried.

"Yes, there is something far worse than mud," Gemstone replied, as his eyes slightly tightened and his lips arched up slightly. He placed his hand back on Marbleman's shoulder and said, "It's so good to see you, my son, but I'm afraid we might be stuck down here for a long time. The brave ones you see in the mud have tried many ways to get out of here, but all their attempts have failed because of the granddaddy of all stealthbills. Why even Moss can't seem to stop it with his freezing Spewing Spar."

A high pitch screeching not to far off broke their conversation.

"What was that?" asked Marbleman, looking upward.

"Yitterbitter, the meanest flying beast of steel ever. It allows no one to escape," replied his father.

Virtuoso gave two pulses of light bursts, drawing Gemstones attention. Looking at the freezing blade Gemstones eyes swelled with tears. Wasting no more time, he said, "I see you have bonded with Virtuoso. I have not been able to tell you everything. I know you have questions. What's bothering you my son?"

"How do you know Virtuoso is its name? I thought I just named it not too long ago? And really, what's eating at me? Do you know everything I have learned in just a few days since leaving home?" said Marbleman.

"Okay, I know Moss talked to you. But remember, you are always my son. I will always love you as my son. However, what Moss has told you, well it is all is true. The king and queen are your biological parents. The king knew you would someday be the master of this special weapon. He wanted, or rather, he wants you to know your family heritage. I'm afraid you didn't name the weapon my son. The sword probably communicated its name to you in your thoughts. The king actually named your Spewing Spar Virtuoso as a spinoff of his name in order to pass it on to you in secret, and to protect you from anyone who wanted to harm you. You are the rightful heir to Crown Glory. The king's full name, that is your biological father's full name, is Vitreous Luster Trueround. I am so sorry I didn't tell you before but…" said Gemstone.

Marbleman gently cut him off. "Say no more. It's okay, my father, I understand. I just wanted to hear you say it was true. You still will always be my father."

"I hate to break up this family reunion and all, but I'm afraid we need to figure a way out of here now, as danger nears," said Moss Agate, who joined the conversation.

"Gadzooks, what the heck is that?" cried out Fragilian.

"It's Yitterbitter, the flying serpent of the abyss. Everyone, get down," warned the old agate.

It was too late, as the beast swooped over them, letting out a bright blue freezing blast from its throat. The blaze cut the boulder in half, just missing everyone.

"Where did it go?" called out Marbleman, who was now separated from all the others, as he stood on one side of the severed boulder.

"There," pointed Fragilian, as the beast circled and headed right back at them.

Moss commanded, "Now," to his spewing spar, which responded with six steady steams of freezing blasts. They hit the Yitterbitter, perhaps injuring it, but not stopping it.

The freezing blasts lit the cavern, allowing everyone to get a good look at the monster.

Holy buckets, it's all slimy black steel with only ice blue eyes and lips. I'd hate to touch that slimy thing, thought Marbleman, as the ruling terror swooped past for the second time.

"No, no, no," came a cry from a nearby boulder top.

Three others, including the guard that fell with them from the trap door, had crawled out of the mud on top of another boulder. Each were all snatched into the mouth of Yitterbitter, as it took them right off the rock top. The dragonesque monster's throat swelled with its skin turning a bright blue, until a blast burst from its mouth, freezing all three of the captives. Then it snapped its huge jaw shut, smashing the three prisoners into a thousand bits of marble.

"Oh my, creature just killed them all. They will never be able to come back," shouted Fragilian, placing her hand over her mouth, as pieces of the shattered rained down on everyone, and the terror of the abyss flew over them.

"That cuts it," shouted Marbleman, firing up Virtuouso to full glowing power. "Over here, you slimeball lizard," he yelled at top of his lungs, which made the Yittebitter make a full turn and charge right back at Marbleman.

Yitterbitter's blast was fast and furious, knocking everyone off the rock top before anyone could even get a freezing sword swipe at it. Except for Marbleman.

"Aarghhhhhhh," yelled Marbleman, as the flying terror sunk a pointed claw right into his shoulder and lifted him off the rock.

"Marbleman," screamed Fragilian from the mud, as the monster of steel carried him higher and higher into the dark cavern and out of her sight.

Chapter 11
Stalagmite Ladder

"Holly horse hockey," cried out Marbleman trying to pull himself off the sharp talon, but Yitterbitters grasp into his shoulder was too deep and painful to free himself.

Still flying higher the terror of the muddy abyss put Marbleman in his mouth using his front teeth to pulling him off the talon. "Ufffff da," cried out Marbleman as the talon slide free. Marbleman fell to his knees on the enormous tongue of the monster as the teeth behind made a makeshift impassable gate. "Virtuoso what are we going to do" yelled Marbleman seeing the swelling throat of Yitterbitter building up with blue freezing power reading to blast him.

"Do something now, or will be nothing but a hand full of dust," screamed Marbleman. Instantaneously Virtuoso blasted out three different colors freezing blasts. The blue blast went straight up and through the monster top jaw right between its eyes. The second deep orange colored blast came out of the bottom of the hilt surging right through the lower jaw. The third freezing stream was pure white surging deep down smashing into the freezing surge rising out of the throat cutting off all of Yitterbitters freezing blast.

"Oh my word," cried out Marbleman covering his head from the blinding thunderous blast from which the shockwaves sent him flying right out of Yitterbitter mouth which was wide open from the overbearing rush of pain.

"Gurrrrrrr," groaned Yitterbitter as he began to freeze outward from each striking point from Virtuoso.

"Virtuoso" shouted Marbleman as soon as his head poked out of the muddy bottom where he landed. "Oh no" he continued looking upward as Yitterbitter's frozen body with Virtuoso still lodged in his mouth, smashed into the cavern side wall bursting with another blinding and thunderous blast into a million pieces of glowing glittering blue ice fragments.

"There you are" shouted Marbleman seeing his sword plummeting downward. Moving the best he could in the mud to catch Virtuoso before losing it in the mud he triumphantly yelled "Got ya," catching the magical sword, which look no worse for the wear.

"That so beautiful for such an awful ending for that nasty creature" said Fragilian reaching down to pull up Marbleman who landed almost right back from where Yitterbitter snatched him of the rock.

"Your injured," said Fragilian seeing his shoulder wound.

"It's nothing it will heal fast," replied Marbleman.

Fragilian titled her head slightly to smiling wide, "I am sure it will."

"What's with all the cheering," quietly asked Marbleman as he looked all around the rock and the muddy waters.

"Why you're a hero, Marbleman. You slayed the dragon that nobody else could," said Fragilian.

Ironstone rushed to his brothers side lifting the champions arm high into the air for all to see in the after glow of the explode creature. From all around the muddy abyss cheering and applauses erupted even louder.

"Well brother I guess this makes you the hero of the muddy abyss," said Ironstone letting Marbleman's arm down and patting him on his back in congratulations.

"Hey," exclaimed Marbleman as his arm rose upward again pulled by Alncio magnetic pull "Hero of the muddy abyss, if your done playing around with flying monsters, we need to concentrate on getting out of here. I have an idea that we can try now that flying creature is gone," said Alnico.

"Darn tootin, let's get out of here," said Ferrite as he lifted Marbleman's other arm with only his magnetic pull.

"What's your big idea? Hey I can't move my arms back down. I don't like it, I don't like it at all," said Marbleman

"Ha, ha, that's what my enemies always whine about in a freezing blade duels, complaining it us unfair that they couldn't move right before I froze their stinking hides," said Alnico relinquishing Marbleman's arm. "Now watch this," continued Alnico taking several steps away with Marbleman watching his arm rising as if it was attached to Alnico. "Trying moving it now."

"I can move it now, but I still feel directly linked to you," explain Marbleman to everyone on the rock who were gathering around him.

"That's right my cousin and I have all kinds of magnetic powers," said Alnico smiling ear-to-ear.

"Don't you see" chimed in Ferrite.

"See what" asked Marbleman?

Alnico replied "Don't you see that we can connect all of us together to make a live ladder to climb out of here."

Ironstone jumped in the conversation "What a ladder up to the trap door? That's really a long way up. Why that will probably take hundred or more of us to get up that high."

"I think that is a good estimate" responded Alnico scratching his chin looking upward at the ceiling hatch far above.

Fragilian shaking her head back and forth while staring at the ceiling questioning "How in the all the World Below would we be able to balance at the top. It would be nothing but a wobbly bobbly tipsy tower of doom sending everyone into the mud.

"That's the whole point, it won't be a wobbly bobbly tipsy tower of anything" responded Ferrite.

Alnico chimed in "We can send different strengths of magnetism pull to hold those more steady at the top or wherever needed in the ladder, yet allow movement when needed. We've done this dozens of times back our village. If fact it is nothing more than a child's game. We called it the king of the stalagmite. Two teams would see how many kids could be connected straight up.

Ferrite added, "Of course the team with the most kids stacked in the stalagmite formation won. As kids there was a lot of shoving and pushing to knock each other ladder down, but we don't have to worry about the here."

"The point is that everyone down here could help make the ladder tall enough to reach the trap door. I know we can do it. So what do you say Marbleman, can you get everyone to help? I think everyone will follow the hero of the muddy abyss," finished Alnico.

Moss Agate moving his head up and down playing with his long old chin beard in deep thought announced, "I think it could work."

Ironstone added "We have nothing to lose but end up either in the muddy waters or to fall smashing into one these huge boulders cracking ourselves to death, ha, ha."

Ferrite pulled his cousin over to the corner of the rock and whispered "Have you lost your proverbial marbles, we've never got above twenty five in a stalagmite formation as kids. How are we going to stack a hundred or more."

"Don't sweat it we were just kids then, we can do this," answered Alnico.

Ironstone asked his brother "what about the trap door, it looks sealed and there must be water on top of it by the looks of all the dripping around it edges."

"I know, we will combine the power of our Spewing Spar's blasting a hole right in that door," said the old agate.

Ok said Marbleman as the two stood together rasing their weapons upward sending two freezing streams straight into the trap door until it burst into frozen shards.

"Look out everyone," shouted Marbleman as ice chunks flowed in the waterfall of water crashing down all around them.

"Nice job son, you two really opened that door. Now if we can just get up there," said Gemstone.

"Everyone in the mud, come to his rock. We are getting out of here." Proclaimed Marbleman.

As the muddy ones climbed one-by-one on to the rock, Alnico took charge "We need to build a circle base as wide as possible on this rock. Largest people on the bottom to make a strong base. Ok you're a big one aren't you definitely will be on the bottom," he said to a large muddy marble person who was climbing out of water.

The rock top soon became busy like an anthill as more and more marble people climbed onto the rock and then into position on the living cone shaped ladder. Alnico and Ferrite positioned themself at the bottom of the living ladder to be able to surge their magnetic pull upward as needed.

"We can do this cousin, really turn it on now," called out Alnico to his cousin on the other side of the circle base, as the ladder grew taller.

A chorus of "Heys, wows, and what the heck," rang out from those already in the living ladder as each felt the strong magnetic pull from the cousins surging throughout their bodies. "I can't let go," cried out one from middle way in the ladder.

"That the idea, your locked together. Ha, ha, there will be no wobbly bobbly stalagmite formation on our watch," gleefully responded Alnico as the formation reached the roof.

"It's a record of all times. There must be 150 or so in the formation," shouted Ferrite to his cousin.

"I wasn't the village stalagmite champion for nothing," joked Alnico with a bead of sweat running off his brow.

"It's time to go," said Marbleman to his friends as the last marble person was helped out of the mud waters.

Marbleman turned to Alnico "Are you alright? Can I help? You look like your beginning to struggle a bit."

"I got this. Hurry get going, my cousin and I can't hold this forever, it's a long climb up," replied Alnico whose face was turning a hot metallic color.

Climbing up on and over the shoulders of a few, Marbleman stopped "Hey, how will we get everyone up the ladder. I mean at some point there will not be anyone to hold the bottom?" he said just realizing this huge flaw in their plan to get everyone out.

"No worries, Ferrite will join you at the top to help reverse the process pulling everyone upward from the top," explained Alnico giving a big smile through his red-hot face.

"Oh, ok," replied Marbleman not sure what Alnico said would work.

Fragilian already climbing next to Marbleman when he said "ladies first."

"Darn right ladies first, I have been down here long enough. Besides it's going to get really dark again down here as old Yitterbitter glowing parts are fading fast. Race ya to the top hero of the muddy abyss" she teased climbing upward.

"Come on father, come you old agate, let's get out of here," called out Ironstone as they all began the long ascent upward.

Marbleman reaching the top first looked back calling out to Fragilian, "Hurry up slow poke." To his surprise a hand was outstretched to help him climb out of the hole.

"Hey there, how you doing my big strong Marbleman, are you now ready to come with me and be mine my love to Tir na n O'g beyond the ancient falls. Come with me now to remain young forever were we will rule as supreme king and queen of all that we see," said Desiree Sappfire lifting him out of the hole and slowly tracing his facial features with her other hand delicate fingertips. Letting go of his hand, she slowing reached for Virtuoso hanging on Marbleman side.

Alluree Sappfire standing further back holding a lit torch chimed in "And where is that handsome brother of yours. Like my sister says I think he would like to come with all of us to land of forever young."

"Oh no, Oh blam damsel no," shouted Fragilian as her head popped over the edge of the hole seeing and hearing Desiree dangerously flirting with her man. Fragilian needed no help out of the hole as she flew at Desiree.

"What the heck is this," said Desiree letting go of Marbleman backing quickly away from Fragilian's two fisted bladed attack. Desiree held up one hand that emitted a force field that effortlessly blocked all of Fragilian blade swiping attempts.

"My, my sweet dear your no match for me. Your especially not good enough for Marbleman as he is going to be the king and you're just a simpleton from the peasant Glass Clan village. Ha, ha you're way out of your class. Ha, ha, escape these halls while you have the chance you young fool," cackled Desiree.

"Well see about that," replied Fragilian as she ran up the wall catapulting over the head of Desiree landing between the two sisters sinking her left handed blade into the unprepared Allure's shoulder.

"Ouch, she stuck me sister. I am going to freeze," cried out Allure.

"Aarghhhh, you lowlife marblerat. You'll pay for that," screeched Desiree who pushed by Fragilian reaching her sister as the two disappeared into the deep dark tunnel.

Fragilian short of breath lowering her eyebrows clenching her teeth looking at Marbleman mocking "Oh come with me my true love to mythical Tir na n Og to live happily forever with me and my skanky sister. If you so like sleazeballs you can have her." She rammed Marbleman's shoulder about knocking him over as she went back to help Ironstone and Moss out of the hole.

Marbleman raised both of his hands into the air saying, "I didn't do anything."

"That's the problem," Fragilian snapped back.

"Well if you two are done with your lovers spat, we need to pull everyone up out of the hole if you don't mind," said Moss although he sense a danger had been lurking down the dark tunnel.

Ferrite was next out of the hole yelling back down, "I am ready cousin, start sending up the people on the bottom first." Everyone waited seemly a long time until the first of the big muddy one from the base crawled up the stalagmite formation and out of the hole. Then one after another they all climb out with Alnico being the last in the magnetic chain. "Ha, ha I told you all we could do it. We are out" triumphant proclaimed one tired Alnico.

"We are out of the muddy abyss, but we are far from being out of Granite Death Halls. I afraid nothing looks the same to me anymore. I don't know where we are in the tunnels," explained Moss Agate.

"What about the King and Queen, we can't leave them in these dungeons. How will we ever find them? Poor Queen Ruby, she got separated from us, I wonder where she could be?" questioned Fragilian.

Gemstone entered the discussion, "Moss have you told Marbleman how the family Spewing Spar, Virtuoso, is connected mind, body, and sprit to all member of the family?"

"Of course, that is how we will find the king in this labyrinth of dark halls," replied Moss.

Ironstone added, "I don't get it, Virtuoso is connected to the family what does mean."

"It means my fine young lads that Virtuoso can guide us to the king," replied Moss put one arm around Ironstone and Marbleman pulling them close to him.

"How," asked Marbleman?

"Just hold Virtuoso out asking it in your mind to find the king. It will guide you," answered Moss.

Ok Virtuoso, you heard the old agate. Do your stuff, find the king, thought Marbleman hold his weapon outward.

"Hey are you just moving that blade on your own brother or is it really working" asked Ironstone as the sword lit brightly pulling Marbleman's arm forward.

"It's working" replied Marbleman as the whole crowd slowly followed behind him down the hallway.

It wasn't very long, just down a few hallways, before Virtuoso led everyone to a closed large solid wood door. "Hey, could the king be inside this dungeon cell," asked Ironstone.

"If he is in there where are all the guards?" cautioned Fragilian.

Moss stood next to Marbleman tilting his head up and down looking over the door and said, "Powerful is your blade. It's mystical powers are beyond are ability to understand. It knows something is in there that will led us to the King."

"Well then, lets knock this door done and get in there," strongly suggested Ironstone.

"Wait a minute, we've done this before,' Fragilian said reaching out to turn the door latch. Adding, "See, it is open, but remember last time a dungeon door was unlocked but it was a trap with Curmudgeon waiting on the other side with an army," as she looked at Marbleman slighting raising her shoulders wonder what was next.

"Hmmmm" said Marbleman reaching to open the door. Squeezing in close together in front of the door, Ironstone, Gemstone, Moss, Alnico, Ferrite, and Fragilian all drew out their freezing blades as Marbleman swung the dungeon door open.

Chapter 12
Gates to Freedom

"Let's roll," commanded Marbleman, as he and his company stormed into the dudgeon room. They stopped inside the large room, looking around for any foe, but saw none in the room. Instead, it glowed from their lit blades but mostly from a pile of royal blue fizzy ice.

"What the heck is that?" asked Fragilian, pointing to the fizzy ice streaks on the floor leading right out another door in the dungeon.

"That, my dear, is effervescent ice from permafrost freezing," answered Gemstone.

Ironstone pushed the pile of ice with his foot. "Perma what?" he questioned, as he tried to shake off the fizzy ice that attached itself to his boot.

Moss answered, "It is the worst kind of freezing. It's a subsurface layer of ice on top of a layer of deeper ice. Think of it as a double freezing, making it nearly impossible to thaw out whoever is frozen inside."

Gemstone laid a hand on Marbleman. "It takes a real expert Nanoite to undo a permafrost freezing. Too fast or too slow of unfreezing can cause both mental and physical damage to the frozen one inside. Or worse yet, even crack the poor soul into to a million pieces."

Marbleman asked, "What if that is the king who has been permafrosted?"

"I hope to the Manifest Power of Peace it's not the King," replied Gemstone.

"Well there is only one way to find out. Let's stop all this yacking and follow that fizzy trail out the door," instructed Fragilian, as she rapidly followed the trail.

"Come on everybody, let's roll," shouted Marbleman, following Fragilian out the door into a huge open courtyard. Far across the yard, in front of a least a dozen rolling marble shapes, gates opened wide.

"There, that must be the permafrosted one inside the rock of ice," said Marbleman, pointing to the large chuck of royal blue ice that continued its effervescing.

"Something is not right. Where are all the guards? This courtyard used to be one of the most heavily fortified places in all of Granite Death Halls. Easily patrolled by hundreds of guards," cautioned Moss, as he looked all around the gigantic courtyard.

"And how did that frozen rock get dragged all the way over there? I'm sure it didn't drag itself," said Ironstone.

Fragilian added, "Why are all those gates open anyway? It's like we are being invited to go through them."

"Something definitely is not right, but those open gates are the way out of here," replied Moss.

Gemstone leaned over to whisper in Moss Agate's ear, "Is that the King frozen in there?"

"I am afraid so, as only a king would yield such a distinctive royal blue color when frozen," replied Moss.

"What are we waiting for? It's a great chance for us to roll out of here before the guards do come back" said Alnico to Marbleman.

Marbleman looked behind him, as the rest of his new hundred plus friends walked out into the courtyard. Turning to Alnico, he said, "It feels like another trap, but I guess we can't stand here all day." Marbleman began to lead his new troop of allies forward.

"It is so good to see all my friends here together for a little goodbye party for the king," cajoled Curmudgeon as he jumped on top of the fizzing rock. "See, he is right here under my feet, well-preserved. But I am afraid he is going to be put away for a long time."

"You permafrosted our king. You low life scoundrel," exclaimed Marbleman.

"You're a fine one to talk. You're the one who struck me down sneaking into my home. Do you know how painful it is to be froze and unfrozen again? I bet not. A spoiled rugrat like you needs to be taught about the real World Beneath," shouted Curmudgeon, pointing his sword right at Marbleman.

"You'll have to go through me for any such lessons," replied Gemstone, raising his freezing blade to protect his son.

"Gemstone Landroller, the always righteous one," laughed Curmudgeon. "I know you anywhere, as Menacing Strong told me all about how you betrayed him, sending him into exile. I'll be happy to take care of you too."

"Gobbledygook is here, as well," shouted Fragilian, who prepared to attack, but quickly abated her advancement when she saw the queen being dragged by Gobbledygook to Curmudgeon.

"I almost forgot. The queen is here for her king, as well as her own goodbye party. She is going to join him in frozen eternity," said Curmudgeon, as he lift the queen by her hair off the ground, with her feet kicking at him.

"Now my boss?" Gobbledygook asked Curmudgeon.

"Now," replied Curmudgeon, waving his glowing sword high in the air and signaling to his hidden guards.

His wave·brought forth legends of guards, pouring out of every concealed doorway into the courtyard. The walkways high up around the edge of the walls filled with guards shoulder-to-shoulder. Twelve rows deep, guards fell into formation, between Curmudgeon and Marbleman, as the gates to freedom behind Curmudgeon all closed.

Curmudgeon, still shaking the queen in the air, stomped his foot, which boomed like thunder, sending fizzy chuck of ice flying in every direction off the ice rock.

"Ooray, ooray, ooray," in unison chanted Curmudgeon's army crouching and lighting their blades ready for attack.

Curmudgeon lowered his eyes, as his mouth clinched tightly, leaving only enough room for him to speak, "You want your king and queen? Come and get them!"

To Be Continued...

About Kevin Edwards

Kevin Edwards is an emerging fantasy author. He has exciting plans for 2020-2021 that includes finishing the fantasy trilogy for middle grade readers called, "Marble Wars."

He lives in central Minnesota with his family and two yipping little dogs.

Kevin is also a licensed psychologist, working at a nonprofit agency to help those with mental health difficulties. Over the years, he has scripted, directed, filmed, and edited several short films highlighting struggles and triumphs that some Minnesotans with severe and persistent mental illness have experienced on their road to recovery.

Kevin is also is member of the local street rod club and drives a 1959 MGA, which was passed down to him by his father. He has also made several documentary short films depicting Minnesotans involved with the hobby of street rodding (one called American Wrench Pullers, three others under Through the Lens, Northern Tin are all posted on YouTube). Kevin has received several local grants supporting some of his artistic endeavors from the Five Wing Art Counsel.

Made in the USA
Monee, IL
01 November 2021